ABOVE
THIS
GRAVE

BOOK THREE OF THE CLOVEN PACK
SERIES

D. FISCHER

Above This Grave (The Cloven Pack Series: Book Three)

ASIN: B074XKX9C9

ISBN-13: 978-1977537256 (CreateSpace-Assigned)
ISBN-10: 1977537251
BISAC: Fiction / Romance / Paranormal

I want to thank my loyal, loving, and patient husband. As I'm typing away with my nose pressed to the computer screen, I feel him staring at me, a smile on his face as he watches me do what I love. He pokes fun at me, making me laugh until my stomach hurts, but I know underneath all that jest, he's proud. My heart swells every time he encourages me to catch my dreams.

I also want to thank my kids, who show me the unwavering meaning of love and the depths of true imagination. I watch them play together on the floor of the living room, no expectations from each other, just giggles and a goal – to squeeze in as much play time as they can before bed. It's with this, that I realize how simple life should really be and how complicated we seem to make it. They show me the true meaning of strength, love, commitment, and loyalty, with no strings attached.

Everything in this book is fictional. It is not based on true events, persons, or creatures that go bump in the night, no matter how much we wish it were...

CONTENTS

PROLOGUE

Flint Rockland's Wolf

He smiles, a metal bar in his hand. *Alpha George Kenner*, my human side provided me in his earlier thoughts.

Peppermint. He smells of peppermint.

Committing the smell to memory, I growl inside my human. Alpha presents a threat, walking toward us. His weapon shines in the dim light, his fingers curl tighter around it, knuckles straining against his skin.

My human is bound, foggy, sedated. He's angry, leery, determined.

My hackles raise. I feel white hot anger. Each step he takes, my growl is louder, my nerves tingle.

Human sends calm vibes. He wants control. I disagree, pawing inside him, expressing my displeasure.

George takes one more step. My attention flicks between his posture and the shining metal bar. He speaks to my human. The bar raises higher when my human doesn't respond. I snarl, ripping against the barrier which keeps me inside.

The bar swings. My pack mate shouts beside my human, confined to his own chair.

I freeze.

Crack.

It connects to my human's leg. I feel the pain, the bone breaking. My human yells, his shouts and pain spiking my rage.

Pawing my internal space, my lip curls, and I dig my teeth into the barrier with all my strength. Ripping, snarling, slamming. Determination. Protection. *Must avenge.*

I shift without my human's consent. The bones crack, reshape, and reconnect with quick speed. I leap from the chair as soon as I'm whole. The metal chair crashes against the floor, echoing, offending my sensitive ears. My muscles contract and I barrel toward the peppermint-scented enemy. Air ruffles my fur, my underbelly. My teeth bare, snarls ripping from my chest. His eyes grow wide, shiny, the skin wrinkled. He swings the metal bar as I leap, connecting with my side.

Crack.

Instant pain blossoms from the area. It spreads to my side, my insides. I fly through the air—objects, people, passing by as a blur. The metal wall echoes as I hit it and drop to the hard floor.

Throbbing pain. Shouting. My ears ring. The shuffle of feet, running. A small whine travels through my nose. My breaths heavy, feet under me, I lift myself. My head whips to the man, my body a little slower. My muzzle pulled back, canines exposed. I stalk forward, a slight limp.

Peppermint man yells at the other men. My eyes sweep the scene as they scurry. A frightened woman slips out the door. Pack mate sits frozen in his chair. Moisture gathers under his eyes. Men shift, discarding their clothes to the floor.

This is my chance.

I leap into the air, straight for the peppermint man.

He drops the bar, steps to the left, grabs my fur, slams me down. His fingers are firm, painful. A bone cracks. The air leaves my body. I wheeze, fighting to breathe.

He takes several steps back, his smell less heavy as he does. I stand on shaky legs, growls vibrating my sore ribs. I keep my head lowered, twist to face him, hackles raised. He smirks. His wolf shows as his eyes glow.

Three wolves skid to a halt in front of their alpha. Dust specks scurry to the air—swirling, swaying, distracting.

My eyes shift between the three. Pack mate shouts for me to stop. I ignore him. Saliva drips from my teeth. The droplets splat to the floor.

Vengeance.

Human watches inside me. His anger is my own. His pain is my own. His determination is my own.

Their hackles raise and one steps closer. My eyes zoom in on him, watching his body, his movements. I dip my body lower, ready to spring. I glance at the door. Two wolves guard it. *No escape.*

The wolf takes a step closer and I lunge. Clash of bodies. Clash of fur. I bite his face, his neck. Blood soaks my tongue. The taste of iron slips down my throat. Our growls vibrate my ears.

We release each other, our teeth clanking. We tumble and land on our feet. He grabs hold of my shoulder and I whip around. Sliding across the floor, his paws gain purchase and he barrels toward me again. I bare my teeth and dig them into his shoulder. Another taste of blood.

He grabs my leg. I yelp, releasing him. Another wolf joins—his teeth sear into my rump. I howl. Another set of teeth slice through fur and skin over my broken ribs. I drop to the ground. The weight is too heavy. The bites are too much. The pain is too intense.

Yelping and whining, I try to wiggle free from their grasps, from their bites. Blood soaks the ground, my back easily slipping along the floor.

Snarls, hot breath, sharp bites of pain. I howl.

Teeth snap. Saliva and red, thick liquid splatters and sprays.

So much . . . pain.

Darkness spreads across my vision.

*****

My eyes blurry, my brain foggy. Snow slick across my wet fur. I blink. Winter snowflakes in thick ribbons sting my dry nose. The wind howls.

A blizzard. I'm outside. I'm moving.

My head lifts, my eyes rolling.

Fight it, my human shouts at me. He beats at my insides.

I'm being dragged, no longer in the shed. The thick blankets of snow are cold on my wet fur, skin, wounds.

Weak. I'm weak. So tired. My head slumps, my vision dark.

*****

My nose twitches, my ears along with it. I open my eyes. I'm in a smaller shed, slumped in a corner. Heavy dust tickles my nose, the scent tinged with iron.

Eyes flick to figures in the corner, I release a weak growl. They remain a statue, but their sneers tell me I'm their prisoner.

Minutes, hours—I'm not sure how long—passes. I fall in and out of darkness, growling when I can muster it.

I jump, my heart thudding fast when the doors open. I growl.

Both my guards rush out the door, their lips curled. Commotion outside, skin hitting skin. My muscles quiver, my cold body. Snowflakes float in through the door. I weakly shift my weight, my fur frozen to the pool of blood beneath me.

A white blur barrels into the shed and skids to a halt.

Brenna, my human breathes. He sighs with relief.

I growl at the female white wolf. I scent her, recognize her, but continue my growl. *Trust no one.*

The white wolf stands as a statue, eye zooming around my body.

That's our beta, my human barks at me. *Let me shift back!*

My eyes narrow. I ignore my human. I can't. The threat isn't over. His safety—our safety—our survival at the forefront of my mind. I lift my lips, growling with the last of my strength.

Trust no one, I growl at my human. I feel him tense inside me.

CHAPTER ONE

Flint Rockland's Wolf

Two weeks after capture . . .

I pant and pace, a limp in my step. It's not hot in this room, but I remain anxious just the same. My stomach grumbles. The beta female is late with my meal.

I pause mid-step to look out the window. The sun is shining on the snow, reflecting a blinding light. I want to pounce on it, but danger could lurk out there. Danger. So much danger.

I shake my fur. Wounds are still healing. Still painful.

A sound in the other room jolts my heart. My hackles raise and I growl warnings.

My beta female appears behind the bars my pack placed in the way of my exit. I sniff the air, scenting for danger.

She speaks soft words to me, but I'm too consumed in my growling to pay attention. I paw the ground.

Leave. Leave, leave, leave!

She wraps her fingers around the bars. I lunge, snarls ripping through my throat. She ignores it and sits on the ground, peeking through my metal confines.

After minutes of watching me, she drops meat inside my big cage. She stands, wipes water from her face, and leaves.

Flint Rockland

I mentally beat against the barriers on the inside of my wolf until I swear I taste blood. He won't let me surface, believing he's keeping me safe. He's traumatized and I don't know how to help the creature.

For Christ's sake, you're growling at Brenna, I shout at him. How can I reason with my wolf if he's finding pack mates—Brenna, of all people—threatening?

That's my beta female, fucking asshole! Let me shift!

He ignores me, even when I scream. I continue to threaten my wolf, and still, he refuses to listen. He doesn't care. In his eyes, he's keeping us safe.

I watch through my wolf's eyes as Bre speaks to me. "Flint, come on. Fight him," she whispers. "You have to be okay. The others . . . They're talking about what to do with you if you're wolf—" She swallows. "If your wolf goes completely rogue. . . if you can't return." Moisture gathers in her eyes. "Please, Flint. I'm begging you."

She grips my bars and my wolf lunges at her for the intrusion of his space. She doesn't flinch though. She's used to his determination to see everyone and everything a threat.

I study her face and feel my heart throb. Her eyes are haunted with dark circles under them. She isn't sleeping well. But what affects me most is the mating bite on her neck. It's fading to a permanent scar.

I've been losing track of time, unaware of how long I've been trapped. The shade of that scar tells me it's been a couple weeks. *Weeks.*

I watch her stand, tears rolling down her cheeks. She throws my wolf fresh raw meat and turns to leave.

No! No, don't go! I scream in my wolf's head. I slam my fist against the barrier again, and again.

Irene Scott

I struggle in my handcuffs as we drive through a bumpy gravel area. Blindfolded and desperate for answers, I ask, "What's going on? Where are we?"

The man driving the car shifts into park and I attempt to squint through the black mask over my head. In this dark car and with the late hour, it's useless trying to catch a glimpse of our location. I've tried using my shoulder to shimmy this mask up, but I can't scoot it past my nose.

"The Castle," the man snarls, unwilling to provide more information. His voice is like sandpaper, deep and rumbling, caused by his addiction to cigarettes. The smell wafting off his skin is unmistakable. It clings to the interior of this car.

After leaving the Cloven Pack territory an hour ago, I had pulled over to the side of the road in favor of helping two men. They seemed to be having car trouble and I had planned to offer them a ride into town. As I climbed out of my car, I got a whiff of them—both wolf shifters—before I was rushed and nearly tackled to the ground. They handcuffed me and placed this mask over my head. I didn't even have time to process the situation I was finding myself in. I was shoved into the backseat of their car and told nothing. Only one of the men had entered to drive this prison-on-wheels to my unknown destination—and probable fate. I had heard the other climb into mine. Whatever they have planned, they don't want anyone to know about it.

I hear the leather squeak of the driver's seat. The driver's side door slams as he exits, rocking the entire vehicle. Gravel crunches with each of his footsteps, and then he yanks open my door. He pauses—I'm sure to take in the sight of me and my attempts to remove my mask—and I whip my head this way and that, scenting the air. His threatening growl startles me and I shrink a little into my seat.

Roughly, he pulls the mask off my head. My gaze immediately shifts to my surroundings. The dark sky stretches above, and the moon shines brightly across the area. We've parked in front of a large off-white shed surrounded by tall shadowed trees. I would have guessed this place once held farming equipment inside, but I get the feeling we aren't here to stir the ground and plant some seeds—it's still winter.

The words pop out of my mouth before I have time to filter them. "This doesn't look like a castle."

"Shift to your wolf and I'll kill you before you can sprout fur," he snarls, then yanks me from the backseat.

His brown hair appears black in the dark night, and his nose is crooked from one too many breaks. His shoulders are broad and lined with muscles, but he doesn't move as gracefully as his physique would suggest. When he had walked across the gravel, I heard a limp in his step. Between the healing cut on his forehead and the injured leg, I mentally tip my hat to whoever got the better of this guy. I hold no sympathy for my abductor.

I hear a car's wheels crunch across the gravel driveway behind us, and I turn my head to it. The other man driving my car parks it behind the one I just exited. He climbs out with a toothy, sadistically excited grin. He's a dirty man with grease stains all over his arms and clothes. I can only imagine the damage he did to my leather seats.

"What are we doing here?" I ask as the limping man drags me toward the large shed. My feet have difficulty matching his long strides and I stumble over the rocks beneath them.

"The One wants to have a little chat," the dirty man says, jogging to catch up to us.

I angle my body to walk faster instead of being half dragged. "The One?" I frown, staring at the building they call 'Castle.' Is this some kind of God they worship?

The dirty man responds with hushed giggles, making him seem more scrawny and repulsive than my original assessment. He reminds me of a hyena.

The large metal door slides open before either of the men have a chance to do it themselves. Light bathes the rest of our path and the full view of what's inside yawns in front of me.

To my surprise, it's a home. A makeshift living area is off to one side. A handful of wolf shifters—mostly males but a few females are sprinkled throughout—lounge on mismatched furniture. They turn their heads in our direction as we step through the door. None greet us.

A small kitchenette and a large dining table are off to the other side. Taped on the wall of the kitchenette and dining area are several pictures, blueprints, and maps.

I release a heavy sigh. Electric heaters hum throughout the space and heat curls around the tip of my ears as I study what surrounds the main space. Cubicles are formed with makeshift walls that are normally seen in business offices. *Bedrooms*, I realize when I catch a glimpse of the unmade bed inside the nearest one.

My attention turns back to the wolf shifters who watch me with interest while the dirty man jogs to the back of the shed and disappears into a cubicle. I wait impatiently for him to return, jingling my handcuffs in discomfort.

A bad feeling slithers in my gut. I don't like this one bit.

A platinum blonde woman exits the cubicle, sliding a bracelet on her wrist as she walks. High-heeled shoes are strapped to her feet and they click against the concrete as she heads my direction. The dirty man eagerly follows behind her.

Once she's standing in front of me, she assesses me from head to toe with a sly smirk. The woman is pretty, but not in a natural way. Her real skin tone and features are hidden under layers of cosmetics, expensive clothes, and several jeweled accessories.

Her eyes finally reach mine and I fidget under her gaze. I feel cornered. Trapped. I suppose I am.

"Irene," she says, void of emotion.

I clear my throat. "Erm . . . Yes? Are you . . . ah . . . " I search my memory, trying to remember the name my abductors used.

She lifts a perfectly shaped eyebrow. "The One." She gingerly holds out a hand and her rings glitter in the dim light.

I blink at the diamonds and then blink at her. *A snake*. She doesn't need to look like one to be one. This woman, who calls herself The One and lives in 'The Castle' surrounded by dirty men and women housed in bedrooms that look like cages . . . What in the world have I walked into? And what could they possibly want with me?

I jingle the metal dangling from my wrists again and lift my eyebrows high on my forehead. She snaps her fingers and points to the handcuffs. Nobody responds.

"Zane!" she barks. My heart skips a beat at the sudden outburst. She gestures to my handcuffs again. An impatient, yet murderous look hardens the skin around her eyes and mouth, twisting her features into something vile.

She crosses her arms while the brunette male standing guard of me frees my wrists. She offers her hand a second time, my dark skin a stark contrast to hers as we grasp one another's hand in greeting. I scowl as I realize I'm shaking hands with the one responsible for my abduction.

"What pack is this?" I ask her, the dirty man, and Zane.

She produces a smile that doesn't quite reach her eyes. I get the feeling she doesn't like to be questioned, even if they're valid ones. By the way she grasps my hand, I can tell she's a submissive wolf. More submissive than me, in fact. I'm having a hard time coming to terms with the fact that she seems to be what they worship.

"This isn't a pack, darling. These wolves," she sweeps her arm across the room, "are free wolves."

My eyelids flutter as I catch the eyes of each wolf shifter staring at me. "You mean rogues?"

She holds up a finger and corrects me in a matter of fact tone. "Free."

"Right," I whisper awkwardly. A wolf shifter with no pack is a rogue. This is clearly a pack. How she's convinced otherwise is beyond me. They may not be able to communicate telepathically because she isn't a dominant alpha, but she's clearly the one in charge.

I bite down on the inside of my cheek instead of voicing my opinion. These men and women are already unbalanced. There's no point in antagonizing them. I'm far outnumbered.

She sways her hips as she circles me. "Irene Scott, the Riva Pack midwife," she begins. I swivel my head to keep an eye on her. "I hear you have a brother."

"Drake?" I ask, confused about where this is going.

A smile lights her face. "That's the one." She reaches the front of me and continues, "I ordered these two fine men to bring you here. I have a proposition for you."

I lift an eyebrow. "I was abducted. Somehow I don't feel like I'll have a choice to accept it or not."

The smile leaves her lips and the murderous look returns. "You're right. You don't. I have a problem, and so far, no one has been able to fix it."

I cross my arms over my chest, uncomfortable. "And you think I can?"

She gingerly places her hands on her hips. "I do. You've got a window that I need to climb through." She lifts her hand and waves it in the air at my confused expression. "Metaphorically, of course. Please try to keep up, darling. It would be dreadful if I grew tired of having to explain myself."

"I'll do my best," I say slowly.

"My old pack has done me wrong. You're going to give me what I want." She inclines her head. "You're going to make it right."

I chuckle at her order. "And who's this pack?"

"The Cloven Pack," she growls with disgust, her top lip curling.

My arms drop to my side as recognition clicks, and my heart thumps hard enough that blood rushes to my cheeks. "You're Jazz."

Zane wraps firm fingers around my upper arm and spins me to face him. "You will address her as The One," he snarls before backhanding me.

My head whips to the side from the force of the strike. I leave my head tilted, my hair covering my glowing eyes while I wipe the blood from the corner of my mouth. I take a moment to calm my wolf who's threatening to surface.

"Enough, Zane," Jazz says in a quiet but cheerful voice.

I turn back to face her, glaring at Zane before doing so. "You've heard of me. Excellent." She claps her hands together once, the sound echoing through the space.

I've heard of her alright. She started the entire mess that the Cloven Pack is dealing with. They've been searching for her for months.

"What do you want from me?" I grumble.

"I want intel."

I wipe the blood again. "And if I refuse?" I look at the blood smeared on the back of my hand. It nearly blends with my dark skin. "If I say no?"

Jazz tilts her chin toward the dirty man behind her. "Luke, would you be a dear?"

He grins, jogs backward, then fully turns and disappears into a cubical.

"Sweet, Irene," Jazz tsks. "You'll be pleased to know we found your dear Drake. He's quite the rebel, you know. Took down several of my wolves before they could restrain him."

This time, my heart skips a beat and every inch of my limbs tingle with fear. I have a feeling I know where she's going with this. I haven't seen my brother in years. He left the Riva Pack long ago.

Luke drags someone out of the cubical. The man stubbles as if he's too weak to properly walk. "Ahh, there he is," she says with excitement.

I mouth my brother's name.

Drake, with several open cuts, some fresh and some old, looks around at his surroundings with bruised eyes. His arms are bound and a cloth gag is shoved between his teeth.

My fingers itch to reach for him, but Zane twirls my cuffs, a warning to keep my distance. Drake looks much older and wilder than I remember. The sight of his injuries causes my wolf to bang against the walls inside me, begging to be released for retaliation.

"Drake, say hello to your sister," Jazz says, placing her hands on her hips again. A pleased smirk lights her face. She's enjoying this.

"Drake," I whisper. Warning forgotten, I reach out to touch him but Zane yanks me back. My shoulder pops from the action and I snarl my displeasure.

Drake stares at me with desperate, broken eyes. He isn't concerned for his well-being, but instead, for mine. Neither of us should be here, but neither of us are in the position to leave.

It's funny how I felt so much braver moments before I learned I wasn't alone, surrounded by rogues.

My brother scans the wolves around him as he tries to grasp the reason as to why I'm here. Once his eyes land back on mine, they plead with me. Not for his own rescue. No. He's pleading with me to run - to flee and leave him to whatever fate they have in store for him. I swallow thickly and subtly shake my head.

"Excellent," Jazz says, clapping her hands together. "Now that everyone is reunited, shall we begin negotiations?"

CHAPTER TWO

Flint Rockland's Wolf

One month after capture . . .

My beta male holds up his hands as he speaks. Growls rip through my chest. Saliva drips from my teeth. He stares with narrowed eyes and assesses the bars. Wrapping a hand around them, he uses his weight to test their strength.

I've tried many times to break through. My teeth marks serve as evidence, marring their silver surface.

I snarl louder and bark a warning. I don't want him to enter. This is my den. *Mine.* My safety. Staying here, we remain safe. My human remains safe. I can protect him.

He leans against the wall and watches me. His head moves side to side. My head follows his movement. His chest rises and falls as he harrumphs. Turning to leave, he gives me one more look before exiting from my view.

Two months after capture . . .

Kenna struggles to sit up from the bed and snatch the fetal heart monitor from my hand. Her efforts are laughable, like a bug stuck on its back. I yank the monitor away before she has the chance to reach it. With the cord swaying in the air, I frown down at her.

"Don't look at me like that! I don't hear the heartbeat!" she panics. "Where the hell is the heartbeat?"

Darla rolls her wheelchair closer to Kenna's bed. "Kenna, honey," Darla begins, placing a hand on her arm, "the baby is still little. With all that extra room, they're free to move around. Give it a few minutes."

Daring the alpha female to continue her impatience, I quirk a brow at Kenna. It's a brave expression on my part. This kind of challenging gesture toward an alpha female won't go unnoticed, but I've dealt with scared pregnant wolves before. She'll be no different than those who heeded to my requests.

Kenna chews the inside of her bottom lip—a habit I've noticed she's recently picked up. Darla, still seated in her wheelchair, Evo, sitting on the edge of the bed, and the mom-to-be staring at the wand in my hand, I watch from my peripheral vision as each of them will the wand to pick up the life growing inside her. The breath seizes in their chest as they wait, pitched forward.

"There," I say in a quiet voice to not startle the room. "There's your baby's heartbeat." Kenna, Darla, and Evo breathe an audible sigh and visibly relax. "It's one hundred and fifty-nine beats per minute." Most moms-to-be have no idea what that means, but I find if I provide as much information as possible, it keeps the anxious parents at bay.

My information falls on deaf ears as they contently listen to the soft thumping heartbeat. I remove the wand and wipe the jelly from her skin.

Evo reaches over and touches Kenna's belly. She already has a visible bump there, a sign that she'll be one of those women who carry large babies. I don't have the heart to tell her, though. That kind of knowledge isn't always pleasing for moms-to-be and she seems like she's in enough distress as it is.

Evo tucks a stray strand of brown hair behind Kenna's ear. "Are you okay, baby?" he asks.

Shifting her eyes to the ceiling, she remains silent for a moment. "I will be. There's just a lot of shit going on," she mumbles.

I pause in packing my equipment away and stare at the zipper of my medical bag. I know the real reason behind her stress—well, at least one of the larger reasons. I see it all the time in expecting mothers. "Only a few more weeks, Kenna," I remind her before continuing my task.

Evo scowls. "A few more weeks for what?"

Darla leans forward and taps Kenna on the nose. "Until the chance of miscarriage decreases." There's a thick sense of motherly understanding in

Darla's tone. She has, after all, birthed two children of her own.

Reese, the Riva Pack doctor and good friend of mine, has given Darla the go-ahead to move about the house today. Reese's only condition is for Darla to remain in her wheelchair until her strength is back.

Two months ago, Darla had fallen into a comatose state when Evo had killed her mate, George, in a double challenge. George was the Gray Pack alpha, and I heard it was an interesting match. 'Heard' is an understatement. My pack had talked about it for days.

Darla woke last week, but her strength isn't what it once was. She's lucky to have survived. Not many wolf shifters survive the death of their mate. All things considered, she's handling the loss well. I get the sense that Darla's mate, and apparently Kenna's biological father, didn't treat her well. I try not to pry, but it's difficult to ignore their private conversations when I'm literally standing in the room.

From these conversations, I learned that when Darla first woke, she had spent a couple of days reflecting. I'm sure coming to terms with her past was a difficult mental journey for her to take. She was grateful to have her long-lost daughter at her side and often told her so, but during my frequent visits, her silence stretched on for an uncomfortable amount of time. Reese was worried she'd have to prescribe her medication to cope with the memories that haunted her. She feared Darla was slipping into a depressed state. Shortly after Reese had considered it, Darla snapped out of it.

Since then, Kenna has spent her free time nursing Darla back to health. Her muscles are weak from disuse, and she still has trouble keeping down solid foods. It amazes me how quickly the two women have adapted to the mother-daughter relationship without knowing each other their entire lives.

Darla looks exactly like an older version of Kenna, but their personalities are a whole other matter. Kenna's prickly attitude often causes Darla to physically cringe, but I believe she recognizes that there's no changing someone's personality. This is Kenna, the woman with the personality of a fire-breathing dragon. I have every faith that Darla will get used to it. Personally, I find this spunky trait of Kenna's refreshing. She tells it like it is, and I admire that.

I zip my bag shut and mentally check off my list of 'things to say to panicking pregnant women' and voice one aloud while unplugging the machine from the wall. "You're really glowing, Kenna. Pregnancy suits you."

Kenna drops her hand from her forehead and lifts her head to properly look at me. Her eyes are already narrowed in disgust, and my answering smile does nothing to turn her frown upside down. She doesn't handle compliments well and her reactions are always humorous.

"If you mean the nausea and constant exhaustion, then yes, I would assume this pregnancy is treating me well," she growls. Slapping her hand on the mattress, she fumes aloud. "It isn't enough that my body isn't my own, is it? I'm a human incubator along for the ride."

Darla pulls back her hand into her lap and switches the subject. "I heard there's a wolf here that refuses to shift back to his human half." The wrinkles on her forehead deepen with her concern and, as if she's conscious of it, she rubs at them. "That unfortunate man, trapped inside his wolf like that. I just can't imagine . . . " she trails off as her gaze shifts to the window where the sun shines brightly through.

Kenna turns her already narrowed eyes toward her mother. "It's not your fault, Mom." Her voice softens. "You have to stop blaming yourself."

Kenna is a Queen Alpha. They're rare and always gifted with some sort of extra sense. Personally, I've never met one, but I've heard the tales that they exist. Kenna's extra sense is empathy. She can feel what others are feeling even if they don't want her to. I'm not sure exactly how it works and I imagine it's a useful tool, but I also believe it would be a burden. Knowing that someone is aware of your feelings, emotions, lies, and truths can make any person edgy. I remind myself to be continuously aware of the direction of my thoughts for that very reason whenever I'm around both Kenna and Evo.

When a Queen Alpha is mated, she passes that gift onto the male. There's rumors about that, too. Initially, Evo wasn't handling it with ease or proficiency. He was blunt and confrontational, and he often butted into the private lives of his wolves. Thankfully, he has a grip on it now and has learned to keep his acquired knowledge to himself. I believe his entire pack is grateful for the restraint.

Darla releases a soft sigh. "I know it's not my fault, honey. A part of me feels that way, anyhow."

Flint Rockland's Wolf

Three months after capture . . .

The beta female stands in my doorway, dropping food inside my prison. I growl but chomp on the meat anyway. I keep eyes on her and she talks softly. I quiet my growls, chomping my meal quickly to fill my empty stomach.

My human shouts at me, making it impossible to hear what the beta female is saying. He wants to be free but his shouts are not as loud as they were in the beginning. He tires easily now. I find it a relief. He must understand—I'm doing this for his own good.

Flint Rockland

It's useless. He won't listen to me and I'm too tired to keep trying. I'm disappearing. I know it, but he doesn't. Without me, he'll just be a wolf. A rogue wolf who will have to be killed. I will cease to exist. I'll just be a memory.

Every minute that ticks by I can feel myself evaporating within my wolf's mind. He's my personal hell and I'm drowning inside him. There's no relief—no breath of fresh air. And soon . . . there will be . . . no . . . me.

CHAPTER THREE

Irene Scott

Six months after capture . . .

Kelsey places her mug down and sits up straight in her bar stool. "So, what's it like—the Riva Pack? Is it much different than ours?"

Kelsey and I are having a cup of tea at the kitchen island. Island is putting it mildly. This section of granite counters and heavy stools could be its own continent, it's so large. Glenda, our pack's cook, would be envious of it.

Dyson sits at the other end, drinking his tea in silence while staring at the contents inside his mug. He pays us no mind, lost in his thoughts.

We've been having a conversation for the last hour. She's been quizzing me, interested in my life and those belonging to the Riva Pack. She can be a sarcastic woman to everyone else, reminding me so much of her alpha female, but to me, she's been kind. It's a blooming friendship, one I'm willing to let blossom. I don't make friends easily. I don't open up easily, either.

I tear my gaze from the kitchen window above the sink. The sun's beams seep through it and splash across the floor, and out in the backyard is the alpha pair with their guests. Members of the old Gray Pack have come to visit the territory. When Kenna and Evo finish giving them the tour, I plan to give her a check-up.

I take a sip of the hot brew while I mull over the comparisons between my pack and hers. Turning my gaze to her, I voice them aloud. "It is a little. The Cloven Pack is more of a family unit. My pack is substantially larger, which makes it difficult to be close to one another. Nothing like what you guys have here." I wipe a few crumbs to the floor to distract myself from wondering why Kelsey is twisting her lips to the side.

Truth be told, I'm fonder of the Cloven Pack than my own. Their closeness draws me in, and I find myself wishing for the same assets in my own life.

I don't have many girl friends in my pack, though having limited friends is by choice. Drama and gossip aren't things I involve myself in—I don't have the tolerance for it. But I still find myself missing the rapport nonetheless. This pack gossips, but only to enlighten and always with love for one another. It holds interest to me. A deeper part of me and my wolf are drawn to it.

Having settled on whatever she was thinking, Kelsey frowns. "That has to be hard. Wolf shifters need intimacy."

I watch Dyson shift uncomfortably on his stool before he twirls the string of his tea bag between his fingertips.

Kelsey picks up her mug, takes a sip, and sets it down with an ungrateful thud. A small amount of tea spills on the island. She pays it no mind. Instead, a mischievous grin darkens her considering expression. "You can always switch packs, you know."

My eyebrows lift at the same time my lips smile off to one side of my face. "That's tempting, but I love my pack. I was born there. I have friends there. And . . . family . . . kind of." I pause to scratch an elusive itch on my cheek. "Besides, I don't have a substantial reason to."

Kelsey slumps her posture. "I suppose you're right."

I can practically see the wheels turning in her head. I decide to switch the subject before she conjures any more impish ideas. "Hey, how's that wolf doing?"

She places her head in her hands and sighs, her mood drastically changing. Abruptly, Dyson roughly slides his stool back, scraping it against the wood floor as he does so, and strides out of the kitchen. She lifts her head from her hands and we watch his back as he exits out the sliding glass door. The smell of fresh spring air blows into the kitchen and a few voices from the new pack members drift inside with it before it shuts.

"What's up with him?" I ask.

"Dyson?" I nod to her question. "I'm not entirely sure. He doesn't talk about it. Flint, the guy who is stuck in his wolf? He and Dyson were best friends. Dyson has yet to visit Flint." She rubs her temples. "You'd think after everything we've been through, all this drama wouldn't be knocking down our fucking door every chance it has."

I look back out the window and think to myself, *that's a fool's dream.*

Flint Rockland's Wolf

I stare out the glass window. A few spots of snow still spot the brown grass. Puddles and birds everywhere. The outdoors call to me.

My pack and new strangers roam the brown grass. I tilt my head and study the strangers. My breath fogs the glass. I move over.

A dark-skinned female turns her brown eyes to my glass wall. I perk my ears. My heart aches. We stare and stare.

Mine.

The female's eyebrows scrunch to the middle. She turns to my alpha female, speaking and pointing in my direction.

I whine and pace in front of the window.

Flint Rockland

I no longer fight my wolf but watch his tedious life unfold in silence. He's curious about the new wolves, just as I normally would be. I don't know what this means any more than he does, so even if I had the energy to speak to him, I'd have nothing to say. None of our daily visitors has told us anything.

My wolf's ears perk as his attention zooms in on one particular woman. She's slender, her eyes a chocolate brown. They're so richly luminous that I can make out their details from here. She's staring at my wolf through the window—a curious expression creasing her beautiful face. I mentally sit up and take notice. I feel my wolf's heart skip a beat and his thoughts of possession. I even hear him claim her.

Holy shit, is my only thought.

For the first time in months, I try to break free of my barriers again.

Irene Scott

Eight months after capture . . .

I rest my elbows on the edge of the cushioned armrests, my small frame engulfed in the massive reclining chair. My feet apply pressure to the carpet and I gently slide the chair into a rocking motion.

"You only have one month left until you get to hold your baby, Kenna. I promise, you'll survive it."

The pregnancy is progressing well, but the extra strain on the body of first-time mothers can be painful and uncomfortable, which is her current complaint.

Evo and Kenna have graciously lent me their guest bedroom. They've asked me to stay with them toward the end of her pregnancy so I'm available for the delivery. I plan to temporarily move in next week, and I have to admit, I'm giddy about it. This place is starting to feel more at home than the Riva Pack compound.

Sobs shake her body. She places her head in her hands and says, "I feel like this is never going to fucking end, Ira. I'm going to be pregnant forever and this baby will never come out."

She's been crying a lot lately and it seems to cause her a great deal of stress to be subjected to such strong emotions. She's given me a few choice words every time I visit, trying to blame me for her hormones. Since I'm a midwife, it's nothing I haven't heard before, but from her, it's a little unnerving. I think I'm as ready for this pregnancy to be over with as she is.

I lean back in the chair, continue the rocking rhythm to soothe away the anxiety that's seeping from her to me, and wait for her sobs to subside. I've tried consoling her before and almost lost my hand when she snarled and snapped her teeth at me. The memory of that experience still makes me snicker, but a lesson has been learned. Never give sympathy to this alpha female—it makes the situation worse.

I had just given Kenna an ultrasound so we could check on the baby's weight and position. Everything looks good. Evo is still grinning like a proud father. If only he knew what the next few months were going to be like—endless nights of little sleep, spit-up covered shirts, smelly diaper changes . . .

I smile at the thought of what labor will be like for him. It's always rewarding to deliver new additions to a family—a beautiful and miraculous experience.

Evo folds his arms across his chest from where he stands on the other side of the bed. "Baby, you've made it this far. Surely another month won't be so bad."

Kenna lowers her hands from her tear-stained cheeks and glares at her mate, her mood switching on a dime. "Like fucking hell it won't," she growls. "You're not the one who can't see their feet, receives continuous kidney shots, and eats everything in sight. I can't remember the last time I took a shit, Evo. I don't even remember what my legs look like. And in exactly one fucking month," she holds up a finger, "I have to push a baby the size of a goddamn bowling ball from a very small hole. How would you feel if you had to push a baby out of your dick? Are you going to fix my vagina, Evo? Because you can bet your ass that it'll never be the same." Kenna continues to yell at him as I chuckle quietly to myself, concealing my laughter by averting my eyes and covering my mouth with my steepled hands.

Brenna knocks on the door frame and peers in. "How's the baby?" she asks, walking into the bedroom.

All eyes turn to me. "The baby's good, but Momma is having some issues." I point my steepled hands toward Kenna.

Evo rocks back on his heels, a little frightened of his fire-breathing mate. "It'll be alright, Kenna," he mumbles, unsure of what he can possibly say that'll ensure his longevity.

"Evo, I wouldn't –" Brenna begins to warn.

Kenna throws her hands up in the air. "How can you say it'll be alright? I've read that the pain of labor is equivalent to being lit on fucking fire!"

Evo's face visibly pales and he steps away from his mate.

Bre glances in my direction. "Was Reese able to get some pain medicine for the labor?"

I nod my head. "She's coming again tomorrow to check on Kenna. She'll bring it then."

Today, Reese is here with me. She's tending to Darla in her new quarters and checking her strength. Darla is doing well, but Reese likes to be thorough. If all goes well, Darla can abandon her wheelchair.

Ben strides into the alpha's bedroom and kisses Bre on the cheek. "How's the baby?" he asks the room.

Kenna grumbles and wipes her cheeks. "Will everyone stop asking how the baby is? *I'm* sustaining its life—he or she is fine and happily tucking their toes under my ribs while it sleeps. Because God-forbid he or she sleeps when I do."

Ben tucks his face into Bre's blonde hair, hiding his smile. The love they share with each other is so thick in the air, I can taste it. Envy curls in my gut, and I shove it away before it can take form and alert the empathic alphas.

"Any news about those break-ins?" Evo asks Ben. Ben lifts his head from nuzzling his mate.

Jacob, my pack alpha, had noticed several break-ins in town—both business and residential—and had mentioned it to Evo. Evo had told him the Cloven Pack would look into it, since the pack itself is closer to the break-ins.

Ben clears his throat. "Not yet. A lot of furniture is stolen, but that's all there is to go on. I heard something about a conference table, but I have yet to check up on that. My guess is it's some punk kids looking for a thrill."

"What about the office cubicles?" Kenna asks.

I plant my heels on the carpet and stop my chair's rocking. My heart skips a beat and Kenna glances at me, feeling my emotion. Pushing my feet back against the carpet, I continue to rock while trying desperately to calm my nerves.

The cubicles . . . the cage-like cubicles at the rogue wolf territory. *Could it . . . could the rogues be stealing the furniture*?

Bre leans against Ben. "I was going to go visit Flint," she tentatively announces to the room.

Thankfully, Kenna's frown moves from me to Bre. "Does anyone want to come with me?" Bre presses as I murmur an excuse and exit the room. In the hallway, I glance back to see if Kenna has returned to studying me, but her attention is on her pack mates who are helping her from the bed.

The upstairs hallway is blissfully quiet, but I don't take my time to enjoy the silence. I jog down the stairs and peer into the living room for Reese. I think it's about time we head back.

I pass the kitchen and wave at Kelsey and Darla. They're preparing food for the pack while Jeremy fiddles with a tablet at the island, a beer at his elbow. Kelsey told me he's an accountant, and by the furrow in his brow, he's nose deep in business-related ventures.

Exiting through the sliding glass door, I find Reese chatting with Dyson by the bottom steps of the back porch. As I approach, I hear parts of their conversation.

"Just let me know if you need someone to talk to, Dyson." She places a comforting hand on his shoulder. "I know a few wolf shifters who specialize in trauma counseling. One of our Riva pack mates is one of them. She's a good friend of mine."

I stop a few feet from them and stuff my hands in my pockets. When they still don't notice me, I softly clear my throat.

They turn their heads toward me, but not before Dyson nearly jumps from his skin.

"Sorry. I didn't mean to startle you," I say to Dyson.

"It's fine."

I scowl at him. He doesn't look fine. His skin is ashen and sweat beads along his temples. Perhaps he does need a therapist. "Do you have a minute, Reese?" I ask.

She nods and Dyson eagerly excuses himself. Reese watches him go, her brows pinched together. Instead of joining his pack who are currently making their way to Flint's quarters, he hunches his shoulders and heads toward his own. Evo and Kenna glance at him as he passes but they don't comment. They must be giving him space too, although their expressions show their concern.

"Hey, Reese," Kenna greets as she waddles by. Her hand is resting at the top of her round stomach. Reese gives her a smile in return. It's a distracted one. I can tell her mind is still on the discussion she was having with Dyson.

I turn to Reese once we're alone. "How did her check up go?" she asks.

I massage the tension from my shoulder as I answer, "Kenna has high blood pressure and significant swelling in her legs."

Reese folds her arms across her chest and nods once. "She's pre-eclamptic."

I sigh. "Yeah, I thought so, too. What would you like to do about it?" I drop my hand to my side, feeling slightly defeated.

Reese leans against the side of the house and peers at the clouds passing over the bright blue sky. "I'll talk to her when they're done with Flint. She needs to be on bedrest and take it easy. If she has any seizures, she'll need a C-section.

"This place isn't set up for that," I whisper.

"I know. High blood pressure can get dangerous."

CHAPTER FOUR

Irene Scott

I wait with Reese outside until the alphas and betas exit Flint's quarters. We've said nothing else since I passed on the information, both content to take in the territory.

Once they do emerge, mates hand-in-hand, Reese falls in line beside them. She follows them up the porch steps and into the alphas quarters, striking up idle chatter while she builds to the news of Kenna's condition.

Alone, I take a deep breath. I've been waiting for a chance to do this ever since the wolf caught my attention from his window. He looked so lonely, so desperate . . . so broken. I like to fix things, and I have experience in dealing with people who have PTSD. My intentions are to help this wolf, and just maybe, see if I can do anything for him.

Feeling like a sneaky disobedient child, I discreetly scan the tree line for any watchers. When I'm satisfied I won't get caught, I push my shoulders off the siding and leisurely walk to Flint's door.

From outside, I can hear the wolf whine. I hesitate in turning the knob, though. The metal is cool against my palm, my heart flutters, and my limbs tingle with adrenaline.

This is a bad idea . . .

Pressing my tongue to the roof of my mouth, I open the door. The most pleasant scent reaches my nose. It's not what I expected, and I inhale deeply, trying to name aroma. Cinnamon, maybe? It smells amazing.

The wolf quiets his whines and replaces it with snarls and snorts. He can't see me yet, but he knows there's someone here.

I softly close the door and take tentative steps toward the bars that separate the wolf from the rest of the quarters. My eyes immediately land on the feral wolf. His teeth are bared, but as I watch him scent the air, his growling slowly subsides. He perks his ears and cocks his head to the side.

Bending down to my knees, I sluggishly slide my hand between the bars and pat the ground. I've heard this wolf is dangerous. I've heard he's close to going rogue, but so far . . . he isn't showing any signs of attacking me.

Has Flint gained a little control?

We hold each other's gaze until he takes a step forward. Inside me, my wolf perks up with interest. His large paws pad softly against the carpet as he steps curiously to my hand. He's not as scary as everyone was making him out to be.

After a brief sniff, he places his head in my palm. I frown, but run my fingers through his soft fur. His scent wafts around me – the cinnamon spice I had detected when I first snuck in.

A content grumble vibrates from his chest and the heat coming from his body seeps to my bones.

Without thinking, without conscious effort, I find myself compelled to join him. So much so that I'm unlocking his cage before I realize what I'm doing. He curiously watches me as the padlock thuds to the carpet.

I swing the bars open and take a step into his space.

Flint Rockland

My wolf's heart pounds a loud rhythm. It's like the bass of a bar's speakers – as if I'm sitting right next to one of those speakers, forced to endure the song to the fullest extent. But it doesn't bother me.

I remember this woman standing outside. I remember what my wolf had called her. And now, here she is, stepping into the room my wolf has been locked inside for . . . I don't know how long. She has our full attention. Her presence makes me feel more alive than I've ever been, and I wait anxiously to see what my wolf does.

45

I watch, slightly fearful as she leaves the gate open at her back. I try to contain my fear so it doesn't frighten my wolf, but he doesn't seem to notice. In fact, all the walls he's mentally built to keep me in are wavering and unsteady.

I mentally shake my head while she holds his undivided attention and carefully ease my way past these barriers. She swats and runs her fingers through his fur again, speaking soothing words to him.

Slowly, carefully, I feel him retreat into me as I surface. Shock crosses the woman's face as my bones crack and reshape into my human form. Normally it doesn't hurt when I shift. It never used to, anyway. But now, after months of being nothing but a blimp in my wolf's mind, my muscles scream and my bones throb during the transformation.

Now fully human and naked, I pant and stare at the carpet in my bedroom through my own eyes. I pay close attention to my wolf, making sure he's content with the retreat. Once satisfied he isn't going to fight back to the surface, I tip my head up and stare at those fear-filled liquid-chocolate eyes.

"How is this —" she breaths.

Shakily, I reach up and touch her full bottom lip with the pad of my thumb. A thrill runs through her skin to mine, something unexpected and unexplainable. My heart swells, filling an empty void as I memorize the feel of her skin. It beats faster with each slide of my thumb, reminding me how close I was to the edge—how close I was to losing myself . . . *my life.*

Shocked with fright, she doesn't move, but her eyes soften at the comforting gesture. The pull to her is like one I've never felt. Every part of her calls to me. My heart slows, sinking to the rhythm of the pulse visibly throbbing on her neck.

I lean forward and brush my lips against hers, needing to taste her . . . needing to see if her lips are as soft against mine as they were against my thumb.

At first, she doesn't respond, and I begin to doubt this weird connection between us. But then her eyelids flutter closed and her lips move against mine. We exhale a contented sigh, our breath fanning over each other and mingling in our immediate space. Her scent swirls up my nose on an inhale, fogging my thoughts and bringing life back to me.

My hand reaches up to the back of her neck and I tilt her head to deepen the kiss. Shifting my weight, I move up on my knees and tower over her. I barely feel the strain of my unused muscles, too consumed with my task, her scent, her touch.

Her hands grab my bare hips as her breathy sighs escape through our joined lips. The kiss is gentle and sincere, but deep and enthralling.

An object hits the floor. The loud thump causes us to jump and effectively break our connection.

I turn my head with reluctance.

Brenna, her mouth hanging open, stands in the open doorway. "Holy hell," she whispers, holding a plate that once held the meat now on the floor. "Irene?" She looks at the woman in front of me. "What the hell is going on?"

Irene clears her throat and removes her hands from my hips. The heat from her touch leaves as she moves away from me. She slowly stands, brushes her pants, and turns without a backward glance. "I better– um– Reese is probably– I should go," she stutters before rushing from my room.

Bre, her mouth still wide open, steps aside to let her pass. She watches her go before turning her wide blue eyes back to mine. "Are you going to tell me what the hell is going on? How are you back? I was just here and you were all growly with fur." She picks the meat up off the floor, places it back on the plate, and sets the plate on an end table in my living room.

I try to stand but my thighs quiver. I grip the mattress for support. Bre crosses into my room, grabs my elbow, and helps me fully to my feet. "Here, sit on the bed. I'll get your clothes." She holds my elbow, bearing most of my weight, and helps me sit on the edge of my bed. After disappearing into my closet, she returns with a pair of shorts.

She bends to the floor and turns her head away from my nakedness while holding my shorts open for me. I gingerly slip my legs inside, the soft cloth soothing against my skin.

Once my lower half is clothed, she stands up and places her hands on her hips. "How are you back, Flint?"

I look up into her eyes, annoyance and exhaustion evident on my face. "Can't you just be grateful I'm here?"

I didn't know how to answer her. Words are failing me. If I told her that Irene had magically lowered my wolf's defenses, enabling me to shift, it would be the beginning of endless questions. I'm too weak for endless questions.

Tears swell in her eyes. The mattress dips as she sits next to me. She wraps her arms around my shoulder and rests her head against my bicep. "Gods, Bre. Why are you crying? I'm fine."

"They were talking about killing you, Flint," she whispers. "Evo and Kenna said they could barely feel you anymore. They thought you were suffering."

I shakily lift my arm and place it around her. "I was," I admit.

She releases me and swipes at the tears streaming down her face. "What happened? What happened at the Gray Pack, Flint?"

I shake my head. "I'm not ready for that yet." Impatience curls her top lip and wrinkles her nose before she averts her gaze to her hands in her lap. She pulls at her fingertips.

It hurts me that I can't give her what she's asking for. I change the subject, instead. "How are you doing?" I wait for the answer she doesn't supply. "You're not sleeping," I add in a whisper.

Still glancing at her hands, she narrows her eyes. "I sleep just fine." She lifts her head and her hair sticks to her damp cheeks. "We're talking about you right now."

A tickle rises in the back of my throat. I cough weakly to it. Bre rushes from the room and returns with a glass of water. The water is cold as I take a few refreshing gulps, and droplets dribble down my chin. I wipe them away with the back of my hand and I switch the subject. "Where is everyone?"

"They're inside the alpha quarters." Taking back the glass of water, she sets it next to my bedroom TV. The concern is still in the set of her eyebrows, and she studies my face. I don't know what she sees there, but eventually her stiff shoulders slowly relax.

I hear my front door slam against the living room wall. The vibration echoing through my quarters makes me wince. I can feel a headache coming on.

"Bre, you okay?" Ben shouts, his marching across my living room audible. Each stomp he takes alerts my wolf.

He must have noticed my gate was wide open because a stream of curses leave his mouth. "Bre?" he shouts again.

Bre rolls her eyes when he stops dead in his tracks in my doorway. "I'm fine," she grumbles.

Ben blinks until a small smile spreads across his lips. "Flint," he says. "You're back."

I nod once. The gesture makes my head throb. "I am."

"How—" Ben begins, but Bre cuts him off.

"—Let's not talk about that right now." She sighs, slaps her knees, and stands up. "Will you help me get him to the alpha quarters?"

I watch the budding trees fly through the window on the passenger side of the car. Hordes of birds flit from one tree to another. Sometimes they fly deeper into the blue sky, acting as one unit, and form a variety of swirling shapes. It's beautiful and captivating. With the open car windows, I can hear their song.

Once we pass them by, I rest my head against the side of the car door and breathe in the fresh scent of wet earth.

"What's the matter with you?" Reese asks from the driver seat.

Upon my insistence, we left in a hurry shortly after I dashed Flint's quarters. I have no idea what happened, how it happened, or why it happened. It just happened. One minute, I entered his bedroom, the next, he's naked and kissing me. And in those seconds that felt like eternity, he had stirred things inside me that I have yet to figure out.

Then, I kissed him back . . .

I grip my thigh as my emotions churn like a storm inside me. I'm not saying I'm not attracted to him, but . . .

He's striking with dark brown hair, a square, sturdy jaw, and his physique is built well. He's the kind of man most females notice, and he probably gets away with just about anything because of it.

I hesitate to answer because I know the truth. I felt that 'pull' and know what it means. Flint is my mate.

My heart should be aflutter with twitter and my soul should be singing. But it isn't. Sorrow replaces what should be the happiest day of my life.

"Let's just get home, alright?" I answer quietly and return my stare out of the car window.

I can't have a mate. I shouldn't have a mate. It could get people killed. It could get me killed. To keep everyone safe, it's a small price to pay.

Flint Rockland

Two days later . . .

I lower myself to the smooth rocks that line the outer edges of the pond and sit next to my alpha female. The sun is setting and the thin clouds crawling across the sky are bathed in pink and orange. It's a romantic sight if I ever saw one. A bit of awkwardness settles in the pit of my gut because of it.

Content to continue watching the newly arrived geese splash in the water, Kenna relaxes her posture and releases a sigh.

"Beautiful," I grunt.

She stretches and then pulls her hair into a bun. "You're getting around a lot easier."

"Am not." I quirk an eyebrow and eye her round belly. "You waddle like a penguin. We've all got our problems."

She slaps me on the chest with the back of her hand. A smile lifts my cheeks and the awkwardness flees.

It feels good that I can be somewhat normal around Kenna. She knows what it's like to go through what I went through. Everyone else doesn't get it, though. They're hovering, like they expect my wolf to take over as soon as they look away.

Dyson, on the other hand, is avoiding me altogether. I know why, and I find it despicably gutless. I figure I'll let him wallow in self-pity a little longer before I hunt him down and confront him myself.

"I do not waddle," Kenna says, forcing a straight face over her smile.

I purse my lips. "You do. And your arms sometimes flap, too."

She turns her head the same time I do and looks me straight in the eyes. Holding them for a moment, her voice turns sympathetic as she lowers her tone. "You don't have to hide from me, Flint."

I sigh through my nose and look back to the water. "I know," I mumble.

Arms folded across her large belly, she rubs absent-minded circles with her fingertips. "You going to tell me what happened?"

I firmly answer, "No."

She stares back at the water with me, but not before I catch the return of her small smirk. "Bre told me about you and Irene. Wanna talk about that?" There's a hint of humor there, an attempt to banish the dark mood mentioning that night has caused. It's impossible to hide my rage toward the events of my torture. It curls around my heart like firm gripping fingers.

I rub at the wrinkles bunching along the thighs of my jeans. "She's my mate."

Kenna's head whips back around. "Your mate?"

I give a curt nod, pick up a rock, and throw it into the water. I watch it dive into the pond, plunging from view like my mate ran from me. The splash sprays droplets in every direction, creating hundreds of ripples that flow calmly to the edge.

"Well, shit," she whispers. "That explains it."

Her eyes bore into the side of my face, searching for answers within my emotions. I shift uncomfortably on the rock I'm sitting on. "Explains what?"

"Her panicked emotions before she and Reese left the house. She practically ran out the fucking door." Kenna chuckles at the memory. "She looked like the damn rabbit from Wonderland. Did she pull you from your dark place?" she jokes, making light of my tension. She doesn't know how to comfort me or what to say, and for that, I am thankful. She's choosing not to pry into what's truly eating at me – into what had eaten at my wolf for the past several months.

"Your feet are swelling at a rapid rate," I observe, changing the subject from my fleeing mate.

It had caused an unsettling ache in my chest to see Irene leave so abruptly. I never thought my mate would run from me when I found her. Actually, I never thought I'd ever find my mate. Many wolves don't. The fact that I seem to be a burden to her is causing a hole in my heart—the same heart she had filled in the seconds we were together. Now, it slowly leaks, causing my chest to ache for the loss of what could have been my future. I try not to dwell on it because I can't explain the void and why I can't seal it—why I can't mend it—without her. I don't know anything about her, yet she's the glue to fix me.

"Apparently," she begins, lifting a leg into the air and examining her swollen ankle, "I have preeclampsia." She explains to me what the condition means and how it affects her health.

I give her a concerning look. "Should you even be out here? I believe bedrest is to be taken literally."

She waves a hand. "It's not resting if you have a hovering mate."

I sigh and shake my head. She's a stubborn woman. By the crumbs covering her shirt, I'm guessing she came out here with a snack as well. Maybe several snacks. Her hair is unkempt—she's given up on her appearance, probably because she feels like a whale. Or, maybe it takes too much energy. I'll never understand the workings behind a woman or what drives their actions.

"What are you going to do about your mate?" she asks while returning her foot to solid ground.

I shrug. "Give her a little space. I'll hunt her down eventually." It's a true statement. I don't plan to let her hide from me for long.

She shakes her head in wonder. "I never thought I'd see the day where the womanizing Flint settles down."

For a long time, I used sex and jokes to hide my inner pain and struggles, and I was good at it. I'm not interested in that lifestyle anymore. I could have died. I almost died. I want more. I want a family.

The sudden urge to seek Irene out causes my wolf to pace inside me, and it worries me that he's so restless shortly after I'm released from my prison.

Irene will be here in a few days, I reassure him. Bre told me Irene had promised Kenna and Evo that she would move in until the baby was delivered. I plan to confront her then. I don't like being ignored, and though my chasing women days are over, I wouldn't mind the chase with this particular woman.

A shiver runs up my spine as I fantasize about the feel of her skin, her overwhelming scent, and how it would feel to claim those lips once more.

Before my body betrays the direction of my thoughts, I ask, "When are the new wolves coming in?"

"In a few days. Ben and Bre have the unoccupied quarters set up. Are you going to go help them move?"

I nod my head, grateful for the distraction. "Yeah, I can do that."

"Good." She holds her arms into the air like a toddler wanting to be picked up. "Help me up, will ya? I can feel my mate panicking like a lost duckling because he can't find me."

Mated pairs have a way to feel what the other is feeling through their connection. No doubt, Evo has tried contacting her through telepathy. By her pinched expression, I'm guessing Kenna has been ignoring him.

I stand and pull her to her feet. She grunts her thanks as I continue to hold her hands until we're away from the large rocks around the pond. When we reach the grass, I release her. She can waddle along without my help.

I stride next to her as we listen to the sounds of the forest. The thought crosses my mind that I've missed her entire pregnancy. A sigh escapes my lips. I hear pregnant women can be funny. Not on purpose, of course, but for the innocent bystanders.

Jeremy's wolf greets us halfway down the path. He licks Kenna's hand in greeting, then continues his patrol. It's almost dark out, and as Kenna teeters and curses at the twigs along I path, I inch closer to her. If she falls, Evo will never forgive me.

It's no longer winter, but a glorious spring. The leaves are already blooming and the temperature is beginning to warm against my sun-craving skin, effectively entering us into storm season. I can't wait to hear the rumble of thunder. I missed eight months of my life behind the bars of my wolf. I've missed so much, that soon, a pint-sized baby will be added to the pack. That, in itself, pisses me off. I can't forgive or trust my wolf for what he did to me. I'm not sure I ever will. Eight whole months . . . A season and a half completely stolen from me. . .

CHAPTER FIVE

Irene Scott

I lay on the bed and stare at the details engraved in the ceiling's texture. Reese has just returned to the Riva Pack territory from a long day of work. I didn't need to look at her to know her hair is a mess and her scrubs are wrinkled. She had headed straight to our en-suite shower without a greeting, and now she's humming a jazz tune I recognize. The scent of her vanilla soap trickles into the room, but the pleasantness of it does nothing to put my mind at ease.

In the Riva Pack, there are too many wolves for each of us to have our own quarters. Instead of a mansion like the Cloven Pack, with separate living areas for each wolf or mated pair, our pack lives in an old catholic school. Our pack had purchased the building and renovated it way before I was born.

Now, each classroom is a bedroom with an en-suite. This place is homey, I'll admit that to anyway. It always will be, but it's nothing compared to the Cloven Pack. My heart longs to return there and my foot jiggles with my agitation for not heeding immediately to that desire.

Reese exits the bathroom, fully dressed and towel drying her hair. "Did you eat yet?" she asks.

"Not yet," I respond distractedly.

She stops at the end of my bed and assesses my mood. Walking over to my bedside, she grabs my arm and pulls me upright in my bed. "Let's go."

I grumble as she yanks me from my mattress, and then grumble some more as I reluctantly follow her out of our bedroom.

"Where are we going?"

"To the cafeteria where you'll tell me everything that's going on in that brain of yours." She shuts our bedroom door and briefly meets my gaze. "You've been acting weird and you've been avoiding discussing it." She turns on her bare heels and walks down the dark hall.

I pinch the bridge of my nose as I follow behind her, desperately wanting to go back to our shared room and go to sleep. Not that sleep would aid me in ridding my thoughts of my mate—he erotically and emotionally haunts me there, too. My heart aches for him, my body desperate for another touch.

She turns to me in the hallway and lowers her voice to a whisper, "Did you hear Jacob went on a date last night?"

I shake my head and she gives a wistful sigh. I'm sure she's wishing she was the one he doted upon.

Jacob is our pack's alpha. Every woman in our pack, and many from other packs, have a crush on him. He's a handsome man in a powerful position, I'll give him that. His dark skin is inviting, and his build would stop anyone in their path. Reese has had a crush on him since before he became alpha, though.

I'll admit, once upon a time, I did have a minor 'thing' for him, too. But once we grew up and he became alpha, I lost interest. Men of power may be sexy to many, but I don't see it that way. Sometimes women have no idea how much time it takes for someone to remain in power. I selfishly want a man who is more committed and invested in our relationship than his power.

I want my life to be more about meaningful connections than governing those connections.

Jacob's father was our previous alpha. A long time ago, his father grew sick. Before he passed away, he made his son challenge and kill him, effectively taking his place. Jacob had been training for it his whole life, but my heart still breaks for him. Having to kill your own parent . . . I can't imagine what that'd be like.

We arrive at the cafeteria and I accept my fate, knowing I'll have to give my best friend the reason for the funk I've been in. It's late and Glenda, having cleaned the kitchen, has already retired to her own activities and agendas for the remainder of the evening. However, we're wolf shifters, and we consume an abundance of food. There are always snacks or pre-made small meals to depend on. Glenda may be a surly Russian shifter, but she never lets us starve.

I begin pulling down two chairs from the top of one of the many tables while Reese searches the large fridge for pre-made sandwiches.

Reese and I have been friends since our mothers sat us in front of each other as toddlers. Our mothers and fathers, all deceased from a fatal car crash when we were young, had told us the story many times.

Reese and I were both crying, restlessly looking to entertain our little toddler minds, when they sat us down together. The instant we saw one another, we started conversing in baby babble. We've been as close as sisters ever since. She's the only one I have left who is close enough to call family.

My brother . . . our relationship isn't the same as it once was. He went to war overseas and came back with PTSD. His personality had drastically changed and he spent many nights venturing out on his own, coming back late smelling of alcohol and vomit and never having a valid excuse for his behavior. He became an alcoholic, and many times, I was left to deal with it.

After I had had enough, I confronted him—told him he needed to stop. The argument became so heated that he left and I haven't seen or heard from him since. At the time, I figured he was finding another pack for a fresh start, but now . . . Now I know different.

My heart skips a beat at the memory of him surrounded by rogues.

Reese breaks me from my thoughts when she plops down next to me. "Start talking, lady." She unwraps a sandwich and passes it to me with a can of dark soda.

I sigh and close my eyes, choosing to leave out my deepest secret of betrayal. "I found my mate."

She pauses unwrapping her sandwich and looks at me with bewilderment. "Who?" she whispers.

I stare at my food, unenthusiastic about answering. "Flint."

She lowers her eyebrows and absentmindedly squeezes the sandwich's wrapper. "The Cloven Pack guy? The one who's stuck inside his wolf?"

I take a bite and mumble around my food, "He's not stuck anymore."

She sets her sandwich aside and turns to fully face me. "I'm so confused." I explain to her what happened, and she remains silent as she listens. Expressions flicker across her features, but they're there and gone too quickly to decipher.

"Why aren't you jumping up and down right now? Why are you even here? Shouldn't you be with your mate?" The disbelief is thick in her voice.

"I can't. I– not right now." It's a long story, and the more I try to form it into words, the more I know she won't understand. Sometimes I don't even understand, but I have secrets and these secrets won't appreciate being brought into the light.

If things were simpler – if my life was simpler – I wouldn't be hesitating. Reese may be my best friend, but I don't share every predicament I find myself in with her. That's not who I am.

She rolls her eyes. "Of course, you can't. You know, it wouldn't kill you to open up to me." She picks up her sandwich and takes a generous bite.

It would, actually. Because if I told her—if I told my best friend—it could possibly mean her death. My death. Many deaths.

Flint Rockland

Consciousness comes and goes. A white metal interior of a van. Bumpy roads. Dyson groaning beside me. My own grunts loud to my ears. Voices—too many voices—as I'm dragged through the cold snow to a shed.

I'm roughly placed in a metal chair next to Dyson. His head rolls as he fights the drug used against us.

Wet, sticky blood freezes to my face. My head rolls to the side. Dirt floors, metal siding, a few featureless faces. I try to focus my vision and wiggle my fingers, but my hands are tied together in a rough splintering rope.

My vision shifts in and out of darkness until freezing water is poured over my head. I grunt in surprise, and my head snaps up. Blearily, I look over at Dyson. His surprised shout from the cold water echoes throughout the large empty space.

My hair is yanked so my head tilts back, and my eyes eventually focus on a man, aging with slight wrinkles and peppered dark hair. He smells of peppermint.

"Do you know who I am?" the man asks gruffly, his peppermint breath washing over my face.

I don't supply answers, because even with my groggy state, I'm unwilling to heed to any enemy's desires.

I'm fully aware of where I am. I know what's happening and why we are here.

White hot pain blooms on my already bruised cheek as the man's fist connects to my face. My head snaps to the side and my gaze lands on a brunette woman. I blink past the stars speckling my vision. I recognize her—her features are exactly like Kenna's.

"George—you're George Kenner," Dyson shouts as George raises his fist to punch me again. I growl and whip my head to Dyson's frightened face.

Weak, my wolf thinks as he echoes a growl inside me, ashamed of our pack mate.

"Very good," George rewards Dyson. His shoes grind along the floor when he shifts back to me. "Where's your alphas?"

Squaring my jaw, I remain silent, unwilling to give him the location of Kenna or Evo. I receive two more punches to the same spot, my bruised cheek hot, throbbing, and already swelling.

I spit blood from my mouth and turn narrowed eyes back to George. He repeats his question and I remain defiantly silent.

George lifts his fist again, but Dyson shouts, "We don't know! Okay? We don't know where they are!" George flicks his eyes to Dyson, and Dyson slumps back in his chair. "They left the territory on snowmobiles. We don't know where they went."

"Shut the fuck up," I growl.

George slams his fist into my stomach. I grunt and wheeze, doubling over in my chair. A few ribs cracked from the force of it, and I close my eyes to fight the pain threatening to take over.

The pain subsides and I open them back up. Dyson doesn't spare me a glance. Instead, he keeps his watery, frightened eyes on the man using me as a punching bag.

"What's your name, boy?" George asks Dyson.

"Dyson, sir," he supplies without hesitation.

My top lip curls and blood drips down my chin. The coward is fucking putty in George's hands.

Inside me, my wolf rages. I do my best to keep him contained, but it's proving difficult. He's angrier with Dyson than he is with being taken from our home, drugged, and beaten in enemy territory, and he throws himself against the confines of my control.

"What do you want from Kenna and Evo?" Dyson asks.

I already know that answer. Dyson must know it, too. It briefly dawns on me that he's trying to keep George talking – to keep his fists from being the last thing I see.

His question falls on deaf ears.

Leisurely striding a few feet away, George takes a metal bar from one of his sneering wolf shifters. He weighs it in his palm before he walks slow and measured steps back toward me. "What about you, boy? Hmm? What's your name?"

Sucking in a breath to ease my ribs, I square my shoulders and tighten my jaw.

George sneers. Quicker than I thought the middle-aged man could move, he swings the bar down on my leg with such force that my silence breaks with a shout of pain. My wolf roars to the surface before I can stop him.

I wake, flying upright in my own bed. Phantom pain throbs in my leg and shouts echo through my room before I realize the noise is coming from me. My wolf, frightened by the dream, howls inside me and fights for control. He slams his body against the barrier every which way. I grit my teeth and clench my bed sheets with my sweaty palms.

As his attempts to break free become painful, an idea hits me. I replace the thoughts of the dream with light ones. The first that comes to mind is my ninth birthday. It had been the first day in a long while that my parents had paid attention to me the entire day. We drove to the river at dawn and fished until the sun set. I remember how the clouds had turned a brilliant shade of orange as we drove back to the pack's territory. My parents' laughter as we sat on a blanket and watched the sun play with the clouds had made me smile so wide that my cheeks hurt the next day.

My parents left the pack when Evo became alpha. My father was the beta back then and had wanted to escape the chaos the old alpha had caused. He was never around, always serving the pack. My mom was the same way—taking her beta duties with a sense of deep honor. While they were busy with that, they forgot they had a son.

They had asked me to go with them – to leave the pack and start over. I chose not to. They weren't admirable parents, and I had no wish to stay in their shadows. I wanted a life of my own, opportunities of my own, and I knew I wouldn't be able to have that if I left with them.

My wolf calms with the memory of my parents' laughter when I caught my first fish. Their joy was contagious that day.

Releasing the tension from my lungs, I yank my sheets from around me and climb out of bed, intent on heading to the gym.

Sweat drips down my back and cools with my movements. I find my gym shorts wadded in the corner of my room, and nearly trip over my shoes in the living room. I slide both on while glancing at the dark lawn outside my window. There's a good hour before the sun rises. With any luck, the gym will be empty for a while.

Skipping the option of a shirt, I step outside and walk into the muggy night air, instinctively scanning the trees for danger as I head toward the gym.

Amongst the darkness between the trees, Dyson's wolf catches my attention. I hold eye contact until he turns away and continues his patrol. His tail flicks as he disappears back into the trees.

I know I'll have to talk to him soon, but I'm not ready yet. I can only deal with one problem at a time. Dyson is lower on my list than my mental well-being. Not to mention actually mating my flighty mate. A little anger swirls in the pit of my gut over that thought. This isn't how mating is supposed to happen.

Opening the gym door, I flip on the lights and head toward the Bluetooth audio system across the room. I plug in my phone and crank the music loud enough to drown out my own thoughts, but not loud enough to wake the rest of the pack. The music pumps through the speakers and some of the tension leaves my body.

Satisfied with the song, I walk over to the treadmill and stretch my muscles while staring at my empty eyes in the mirrors that line the walls. My eyes look ghostly, haunted, empty.

I look away from the man I no longer recognize, step on the belt of the treadmill, and adjust the speed.

I was lucky. Truly lucky. If my dream would have gone any further into the memory, I wouldn't have been able to calm my wolf. I fear that he'll take me under again, and this time, I won't have my mate to pull me out. I'd be in the dark, a black void . . . ceasing to exist.

A half hour later, I'm beating on the punching bag when a hand touches my shoulder. I had slipped into a blissful train of thought where nothing had pressed into my mind demanding attention. I turn the swing of my balled-up and taped fist and connect before I think it through. My knuckles slam into Ben's jaw, and his head barely shifts to the side. The man is a brick wall, and I watch as his eyes glow wolf for a moment before he shakes his head in a quick motion.

"Sorry, I didn't hear you come in," I mumble. I unwrap the tape on my right hand. My palms are sweaty, and the sweat had loosened the sticky substance making it easily removable.

Ben searches my face and considers my words. "I called your name a few times."

I shrug and move to throw the wadded tape into a nearby trash can. "Didn't hear it."

I see Ben fold his arms over his chest in the reflection of the mirrors. "What's going on with you, Flint? Bre's worried and so am I."

I turn to face him and lean against the mirrors, the cold surface refreshing against my hot skin. "Nothing," I say casually.

His jaw ticks from my flippant attitude. "Don't try that bullshit with me," he pauses, his voice lowering. "Your wolf is out of control, isn't he?"

"That's not your problem."

He strides over to me and grips my shoulder. "It is, Flint. He's a danger to you and a danger to the pack." He grits his teeth and speaks through them, "Get him under control."

I shake his hands from my shoulders. "Easier said than done."

"Yeah," he breathes, visibly relaxing while rubbing the tension from the back of his neck. "Look, I've been wanting to talk to you about that. I'd like to teach you Krav Maga." I laugh, a great barking belly laugh. *How the hell is that going to help?*

Ben doesn't find amusement in it, and adds, "My wolf and I—we have a lot of anger problems—" I cut him off again with a snort. I've seen first-hand what kind of damage his 'anger problems' cause.

"It helps, Flint," he mumbles.

I give him a considering expression from the corner of my eye.

"Couldn't hurt, could it?" Ben asks when my silence stretches on.

At this point, what could it hurt? I shrug, my wet shoulders sliding easily against the mirror. "Why not."

Pushing off the wall and grabbing a small towel from the rack, I wipe the sweat from my face and neck.

"Good," he says, removing his shirt. "We'll start now."

I whip my head back around. "Right now?" I had planned to go to the pond to sit and wait for Kenna. We had been meeting there, unscheduled, the last few mornings. She would reflect on her own life while I did the same.

Kenna may act like she's over the torture she endured by her brother, but I know better, and she with me. Her dreams still haunt her, and her eyes still hold that same blank look that mine do. Whether she voices that aloud, it doesn't matter. I'm observant—I know she isn't sleeping well. I see it when her mind wanders, and I know where it takes her, and I'm not the only one who has noticed. Evo watches her closely, too. Not because of the pregnancy—though it looks that way from the outside—but because her thoughts can take her to dark places. I get that.

We sit at the pond for our quiet time—to get away from the sympathy of watchful, weary eyes.

Ben flings his shirt to the side and it slides across the mats, coming to a final rest at the wall. "Yes, right now. I know you and I have had a few rough encounters, but let's set that aside. I'm here to help you, Flint." He takes my disbelief for self-preservation. Lately, I don't care so much about self-preservation, but I'll let him take my tone however he wants.

I throw my towel into the laundry basket and stride over to stand in front of the once-intimidating male. Since I went through what I went through, not much intimidates me anymore.

He quirks a thick eyebrow and studies my stance. He frowns and angles his foot forward, nudging my feet apart so that one is placed back farther than the other. Nodding in satisfaction, he taps his shoulders. "Place your hands here."

I roll my eyes and let out a sigh but do as he wishes. Leaving his fingers flat and palms open, he quickly jabs away both my arms and his elbow connects to my chin before I can blink. I step back, my eyes widening in surprise.

He allows a small smile of satisfaction. "Everything you do, every move you make, will come from one simple fighting position." He bends to my legs and places them in the same position he did a moment ago. Then, he stands up and mimics the same stance, but shifts his body slightly to the right. "Always keep your elbows close to your body and your hands slightly open." He places his open hands close to his face and gestures for me to do the same. "This stance—your feet, your hands—will make it easier for you to adjust to any oncoming assault."

I nod and tuck my elbows in. "Every punch to the face should be here." In slow motion, he uses his fist to fake-punch my eye, nose, jaw, and throat. "The purpose is to neutralize the threat, but keep it simple. Knowing the points of weakness can take down the threat faster than blindly throwing your fists around."

I listen carefully to his teachings, my wolf paying close attention to every inch he moves and every twitch he makes. At some point during the lesson, the pack trickles in, silently watching Ben and I while they lift. I can hear Evo chuckle each time my feet are swept out from under me, but I don't give him much consideration. I'm content with absorbing Ben's movements and storing it in my brain. Blocking out the distractions becomes easier as the time goes by.

At the end of the lesson, Ben asks me to show him what I've learned by using him as a demonstration. "I promise I'm not trying to trick you," he assures through a grin when I glare skeptically. "Show me what you've learned."

We get into our fighting stance and he comes at me, intent on landing a blow to my cheekbone. I swallow the flash of memory of George's fist in a dark shed before it blossoms into something more.

Quickly, I block his fist with an outstretched hand, twist his wrist, and kick out my foot, sending him staggering back a few feet.

The wind gushes out of his lungs and he coughs for a moment, then turns his eyes to mine.

Jeremy whistles in the background as a pure and true smile spreads across Ben's face. He stands upright and twists to stretch his hips. "Excellent."

"I want to spar with him next," Bre demands. She steps away from the lifting machine and drapes her sweaty towel over the bench.

I frown, not having realized that Ben had been teaching her during my absence. I may just get my ass handed to me.

She stands in front of me, her stance as perfect as Ben's.

I clear my throat, a little worried when an expression of nothingness replaces her usual cheerful smile. "Go easy on me."

She laughs without humor. "Not a chance. I've got months of you picking on me to make up for."

CHAPTER SIX

Flint Rockland

I throw the box into the moving van and turn to Ben. "This is it? Only one mated couple and two other wolves? What happened to the rest of their pack?" I wipe at the sweat gathered on my brow. It's a humid day—uncharacteristic for this time of year. My shirt clings to my back and breathing normally is a difficult task.

Standing next to our SUV's open trunk door, Bre places her hands on her hips and scans the outside of the cabins. "What's wrong?" I ask.

She shakes her head. "It looks so different without all the snow. Pretty, actually, if it wasn't marred with bad memories."

I turn to look with her. She's right—it is a nice view with full trees and plenty of frolicking birds, but this territory holds memories none of us wish to revisit. The sooner we get off this land, the better.

She turns back to Ben who moves an inch closer to his mate. Bre adds to my earlier question, "I thought there were more wolves coming to our territory. What happened to them?"

Ben breathes out a sigh and scratches the back of his neck. "I don't know."

A Gray Pack wolf shifter—I suppose he would be Cloven Pack now—walks up to the SUV and chucks his suitcase in. He turns to me first and holds out his hand for me to shake. "Romaine," he introduces himself.

He has Greek-like features—his jaw is square, broad shoulders, small hips, and his wavy hair is jet black. He turns to Ben and Bre and shakes their hands as well.

Romaine fans his shirt to cool himself down and then puckers his Egyptian-ish lips. "We have a problem," he begins.

"The problem being half your wolves disappeared?" I ask, crossing my arms over my chest.

Placing his hands on his hips, he nods and shifts his weight to the other foot. I note the nervous habit. "They disappeared a few weeks ago."

Ben's forehead scrunches in frustration. "And you're just now telling us this? Why didn't you call when you noticed they left?"

He looks to Bre, the most sympathetic of us all combined. "We were afraid you wouldn't take us in."

A red-headed female breaks our conversational circle when she walks through the middle of us. "If there were only a few of us left, we worried you'd send us away instead of adding us to your pack," she says while squeezing a small box on top of the others. Once finished, she pushes her red hair from her face. "Victoria." She waves to our group as a way of introducing herself, then pulls out a piece of gum from her pocket and pops it into her mouth. She chews with a smack and I visibly cringe.

Ben smiles at my discomfort, like he has his own private joke. "Nice to finally meet you, Victoria."

She frowns up at him and shields her eyes from the sun to get a better look. "Do I know you?"

Ben laughs. Hearing him laugh is still so new to me. The Ben I remember was an asshole. Hard and rigid. A workaholic. I blink to the sound of it.

"Not exactly," he replies before turning to Romaine. "Where are the other Gray Pack members?"

Romaine shrugs and stuffs his hands in the pocket of his jeans. *Another nervous gesture.* "We don't know. One night, they were here, and the next morning, they were gone."

I fold my arms across my chest and lean against the back of the moving van. "No warning? None at all?"

Victoria shakes her head, her hair waving. She licks her bottom lip. "Someone was also in the alpha's house. His old house, I mean. I didn't think anything of it until now." She switches her eyes between Ben and me and pops her gum. I cringe again, biting my tongue and holding back unfriendly words about her annoying habit I'll be forced to endure until the end of time. "Can they be related?"

Romaine looks down at her, confused. "You didn't tell us that."

Dismissing his attitude, she shrugs. "Like I said, I didn't think much of it. I went in there to check the message machine and most of the lights were on."

I sigh and turn my elevated eyebrows to Ben. In a disapproving motion, Ben slowly shakes his head. He turns on his heel and strides across the grass to the house. By his posture, he's just as miffed as I am that this pack had kept so much from us without meaning to. These wolves have had no training, whatsoever. It tells what kind of a leader George Kenner really was.

The rest of the group follow, including the mated pair, Jessup and Evalyn. They introduce themselves to Ben, briefly stopping him on his mission to the house.

I wait for a few seconds, listening to their swapped pleasantries and debate whether or not to follow them inside. Curiosity gets the better of me and I jog up the porch steps after them.

When I was brought here before, I never saw the house. The drugs had prevented that. But now that I'm up close and personal to the house my torturer once resided in, I note a few details.

The white house is well-kept. The windows shine in the heat of the sun without a streak on them. The siding is pristine, not a speck of dirt from last autumn. No dead leaves, sticks, or new weeds grow in the rock garden, either. Neatly trimmed and pruned vegetation grows around the house, and the beginning of new vines are already creeping up the siding.

Someone had taken care of this place well. My guess is that landscaping the alpha's house was an appointed duty, and not one George Kenner did himself. He didn't strike me as the type to get dirt under his perfectly manicured fingernails.

Even though Kelsey maintains our landscaping, it's never been an appointed duty. She has never been satisfied with anyone else touching it, which is fine by me. If asked, I'd mow over every flower and bush and call it a successful day. Pruning and trimming are for the birds.

The group left the door ajar and disappeared inside the house. Next to the front door, the gold numbers '3113' are screwed into the siding.

I take a moment to breathe deeply before I follow them in.

The interior is old-fashioned. Antique rugs accent the original hardwood floors, and vases of similar fashion squat on every surface. I swipe my hand along the entrance side table, noting the degree of dust resting there. Since George Kenner was killed, no one had been in this house to clean. This will make it easier for me.

I take careful steps down the hall. The group heads to the kitchen to see if anyone was stealing food, but my instincts guide me somewhere else.

The floor creaks as I stand in the middle of the dark hall and peer up and down its length. All the doors are open, except one. Why one? Why is only one door closed?

Before reaching the closed door, I slowly lower myself to the floor. The sun is trickling in through the other end of the hallway, giving me the perfect opportunity to . . .

Yep, I think to myself, smirking. In a path down the middle of the floor, the layers of dust have been disturbed. Someone had headed this way and entered this closed door. It's exactly where the path disappears into.

I rise off the floor, dust my hands together, and turn the knob. Immediately, the smell of peppermint assaults my nose and stirs a growl from my wolf before I get a chance to look inside.

Flicking on the lights, peer into what's clearly an office. Neatly stacked papers still lay on the desk along with paperweights and office supplies. No one has touched the desk. Why? Out of all the rooms inside this house, why would someone come in here and not go near the desk?

Behind it are rows of books on shelves, organized alphabetically. I walk over to them, angling my head just so, and note that the dust hasn't been disturbed on any of the shelves.

Hands on my hips, I continue to scope out the room for anything out of place. The chairs are neatly placed in front of the desk, the curtains are hung off to the side with perfect drooping drapes. I'm getting the idea that George Kenner was a neat freak.

None of the knick-knacks, as Kelsey calls them, have been disturbed.

Stumped, I frown and visually sweep the room one more time. Nothing seems out of place, everything has a spot, so where . . .

My thoughts trail off as my eyes land on the only picture hanging on the wall. Framed in elegantly carved wood is a picture of George, signed by the man himself. A self-portrait done with precise clay strokes.

I walk up to the large, crooked picture and scan the wooden frame. On the left and right side of the frame, dust has been wiped off in the shape of four fingers.

Grinning, I take the picture off the wall. Behind it is a safe door. "Jackpot," I whisper to myself.

"What did you find, Sherlock Holmes?" Bre asks from behind me. She had tried her damnedest to be stealthy, but I'd heard the floorboards creak in the hallway as she made her way down it.

"Well, mam," I say with a high-pitched female western accent, "I've been a busy little bee and just happened to cross this here metal box." I dip the same tone of voice and accent down to a whisper. "Mam, do you thank they were-a hidin' somethin'?"

"Asshole," she teases. "That's not how Sherlock Holmes sounds." She stands on her tip toes and peeks over my shoulder at the small safe inside the wall.

"I don't know what she sounds like. I don't watch movies," I grumble.

"She is a he . . . and it's a well-known book character."

"He sounds like a she, and I don't read books."

"Ah," she says with a sigh. "Everything that's wrong with you now makes perfect sense."

I roll my eyes and we stare at the safe.

"What do you think is in it?" she asks, her voice sobering.

"I have no idea, but someone else was interested in it."

When the others trickle in, Victoria walks right up to the safe and enters the code. 3113, I note—the same number as the house address.

Gawking, I turn my head and blink at her. "I was getting to that."

"Sure, you were." She takes a step back when the lock clicks and swings open. "It's empty," she voices with disbelief.

I lean against the desk and fold my arms across my chest. "And a gold star for you," I mock.

Victoria shoots me a glare and Bre nudges me with her elbow. A small part of me was hoping for a little buried treasure.

"What was in the safe?" Ben asks, flipping through the papers on George's desk.

Victoria blows out a breath and taps her thighs with her thumbs. "Money, I guess. I've seen him put a couple stacks in there." She looks back at the empty safe. "I'm not sure what else he could have in there. It's not that big."

She pops her gum again and my mind-to-mouth filter evaporates into dust. I growl and hold out my hand to her. "Spit it out," I say between clenched teeth.

Mock shock takes over her face before she drops the gum into my hand with a glob of spit. I stare at it, fighting the urge to fling it off.

"Your wish is my command," she says with a smile.

I growl and search for a small trash bin. When I locate its whereabouts, I dump the gum and spit inside it, and retake my post in front of the safe. Victoria watches me with interest as I hold my hand out in front of her, then squeals when I dramatically wipe my hand with her shirt.

"That's disgusting!" she proclaims.

"What, exactly, was your job here?" I ask, twirling my hand in the air to indicate the house or pack.

Bre cautions my attitude by growling my name in warning. I look at her, the expression of innocence. "What? I wasn't trying to be rude. I'm curious." I shrug and turn back to Victoria. Her hands are on her hips while she glares at me, clearly offended by my question.

"I did the housework for Mr. and Mrs. Kenner," Victoria says, a defensive tone thick in her voice.

I lift a brow. "Is that what you called them?" Even Craig, our old alpha and Evo and Bre's father, never asked us to address him as such. "Did they have you wear the teeny tiny black dress to go with it?"

"That's it!" Bre barks at me. "Out in the hall. Now." She grabs my arm and yanks me toward the office door. She tows me down the hall into the main living area before she stops and faces me. "You don't treat people like that, Flint." She wags her finger in my face. "These are going to be new members of our pack. They've been through more shit than you can imagine. Can you at least be welcoming?" She flings her hands into the air. "I know you're having a hard time with what happened to you here, and then the issues with your mate, but for fuck's sake." She places her hands on her hips. Her face is a light shade of red while she huffs loud breaths and waits for my excuse or an apology.

I don't have one.

I purse my lips, stuff my thumbs into my back pockets, and rock on the back of my heels. How do you answer a chick whose face is as red as a tomato and steam is coming from her ears?

"I have the right to remain silent. Anything I say or do will be used against me."

She flings her hands into the air again and stalks out of the house. She leaves the door open, and I watch her march back to the SUV through the window.

Thunder rumbles outside and a flicker of lightning flashes inside the darkening clouds. I take a deep breath while fighting the urge to smile, and then I follow her.

As I jog down the porch steps, gravel crutches under Bre's shoes. Once she reaches the trunk of the car, she closes the back door roughly while ignoring my approaching presence. Anger still curls her top lip, and instead of trying to cheer her up, I remain silent. It's better to not apologize now. Not when I'm still on her shit list.

Shortly after, Ben, Romaine, Victoria, Jessup, and Evalyn file out of the house. A raindrop hits my arm and I lift my gaze to the low and rigid clouds. The wind picks up as I do, and Bre holds back her hair as she peers up at them with me.

"That's an angry storm," Bre whispers to nobody in particular.

"The fun and games are over, folks. Time to get going," I mumble as Ben passes me. He reaches his mate and kisses her forehead, then ushers her to their SUV parked in front of the one we've been loading with belongings.

Irene Scott

On the Cloven Pack's front porch, I cross my legs on the porch swing Kelsey and I occupy. Jeremy, Kelsey, Kenna, and I are all actively watching a vicious storm preparing to roll across the sky. It's a distance off yet, so we have some time before we need to head inside.

We can hear the threatening thunder and shiver every time a subtle cold and humid breeze slithers through our space. My wolf anxiously pays attention, not liking how eerily calm the woods are. Not a single bird peeps. Not a squirrel forages.

The pack wants to be here when the new wolves arrive. This isn't my pack, but I tagged along out of curiosity anyway. Besides, I can't take care of Kenna if she's out here and I'm huddled inside.

"What time are they supposed to be here?" I ask softly, interrupting the quiet.

For balance, Kenna uses the wooden rails outlining the porch while she stretches her lower back's tight muscles. Her large baby bump is stiff and unmoving as she stretches from side to side. "I talked to Ben a minute ago. He said they weren't far. I guess there are only four wolves moving in."

Kelsey rocks the swing off center when she abruptly straightens her back. "Four?" she screeches. "I thought there were more than that."

Kenna stands upright, waddles her way to the porch swing, and gingerly takes a seat between us. I uncurl my legs to make room for her. "There were. We'll discuss that later." She sighs as she leans back, then rests a hand on her belly. "Evo wants to hold a pack meeting when the new ones arrive." She turns her head toward me. "Are you all moved in?"

"Sure am," I say as cheerfully as I can. A crack of thunder punctuates my words.

I'm at war with myself about temporarily moving in. As much as I love this pack, I'm like it less knowing I'll be living under the same roof as Flint. But at the same time, I'm finding myself intrigued by the idea of maybe getting to know the man who's meant to be mine. My wolf doesn't understand my thoughts and reluctance on the matter. She can smell his scent everywhere and begs me to go to him.

I've heard the rumors about him—that he's a lady's man. That doesn't bother me. What bothers me is dragging him into my shit and having yet another person's life to be responsible for. But my wolf doesn't understand human drama. It's infuriating at times.

My wolf is right about one thing, however. His scent does call to me. And, he's sure something to look at. Hell, I saw him naked. There's not much left to the imagination besides the vivid fantasies that have taken over my dreams.

Kenna wrinkles her nose to my answer. "Your smile doesn't match your mood," she comments dryly.

I shrug, pretending indifference. "I imagine I'll be homesick, is all." She snorts. It's not easy remembering that she can detect a lie. I quickly change the subject to avoid further probing. "Are they going to arrive before the heart of the storm does?"

Jeremy checks his watch. "They really should pull up any minute."

Kenna rubs her swollen belly. "Are you sure everything is okay with the baby? I have such a bad feeling about this." She runs the other hand through her long, dark brown hair and twirls the ends through her fingers.

I place my hand on top of hers. "Right now, there's no cause for concern. Don't panic. There are millions of women who deliver healthy babies with your same condition."

Kelsey looks around the porch. "Where is everyone else?"

"My mom is nesting—she seems to do that a lot. Better her than me," Kenna chuckles. "Dyson is running patrol and Evo is in his office obsessing over the weather."

Curious about the wolf shifter that seems to be avoiding all contact with his pack, I ask, "How is Dyson doing?"

Kenna sighs as she finger-combs her hair into a bun. "He has a lot of regret. Sometimes I feel shame coming from him, but I don't fully understand why. Evo and I are trying to give him some space, and when he's better, we'll . . . I don't know . . . talk about *feelings* with him." I grin a bit at the way she says feelings, as if the word leaves a bad taste on her tongue.

Kelsey scratches her cheek. "I've noticed he and Flint aren't on speaking terms."

"Yeah," Kenna drops her hands to rest on her thighs. "Something went down at the Gray Pack that we aren't privy to because Flint isn't talking either. My mom said they roughed Flint up pretty good but left Dyson alone for the most part. She doesn't have much information—she said she snuck out of the interrogation as soon as Flint shifted."

I look back at the sky. "Going through something like that would strain any friendship," I mumble.

"They'll figure it out." Kenna frowns, and her mood abruptly shifts. "They better fucking figure it out. Dyson's a good guy. Flint knows that. If there's drama going on after the baby is born, I'll kick —"

Kelsey stands up and points. "They're back."

The moving SUV rounds the curved gravel driveway with one more SUV behind it. The storm welcomes them with a crack of thunder and a spiderwebbed line of lightning stretches across the encroaching dark clouds.

Both vehicles park out front and the doors fling open as rain begins to plop heavy droplets across the lawn. Flint, Ben, and Bre hop out of the car and wait for the four new wolves. Seconds later, they rush to the house, heads shielded with their arms.

There's two unfamiliar females and two unfamiliar males. All glance around the territory as they dash to the porch. They stomp up the steps and then flick their hands to rid the droplets beaded across their exposed skin.

The rain quickly turns to pea-sized hail, a stark contrast to the green blades of grass as they pelt the landscape.

One of the females, a petite gal with short red hair, gives a small wave. I'm the only one who waves back, and a blush heats my cheeks for how awkward it feels.

"What are you guys doing out here?" Bre hisses.

Kenna frowns at Bre's attitude. "What do—" Her sentence is cut off when the sirens wail loudly in the distance. We turn our heads toward the sky and study the clouds we had dismissed as nothing but a normal spring storm. The landscape darkens as we stand there, lightning flashing at an alarming rate.

"They're rotating," Jeremy says as he squints at the clouds. I lean into the railing to better peer immediately above while the others watch, fascinated, as a sheet of rain makes its way across the lawn.

"There's a tornado warning. They issued it just a few minutes ago," Bre says.

"We should move inside," Ben orders.

Nodding, Bre grabs Kenna by the elbow and steers her toward the front door. I hold back while the others follow her, content with being last in line. These sorts of storms don't scare me, and even if there is a tornado, there's a small chance this pack home will be in its path. At least, that's what I'm telling myself.

Turning away from the rail, I straighten my shirt as my eyes catch the gaze of my mate. He remains on the porch while the others file inside. I hold my breath under his wordless attention, his arms dangling loose at his sides. His damp shirt clings to his muscles, and the sight of them, I shiver.

At first, Flint hesitates, wrestling with his own thoughts and desires, until finally, he approaches me. He raises his hands up, like he's talking to a frightened deer. "Irene—" he begins.

I angle my body toward the open front door, diverting my gaze entirely. "We should go in the house," I mumble. My wolf rustles uncomfortably as I turn my back on my mate and slowly stride inside. The heat of his attention on the back of my neck doesn't go unnoticed, and his disappointment doesn't go unfelt. But I can't involve him in my messy life. If he knew – if I told him about the mess I'm in and how I can't be his mate because of it, he wouldn't understand. It would only make matters worse.

CHAPTER SEVEN

Flint Rockland

I follow Irene behind the rest of the pack as everyone makes their way to the kitchen. Evo's footsteps rumble down the second-floor stairs at the same time Dyson, in only a pair of shorts, walks through the sliding glass doors off the dining room. Dyson drips rain, his hair plastered to his scalp. I pay little attention to him.

Bre leads the group past the island. Darla is seated on one of the stools with a glass of wine resting on the island's surface. She slides off the stool, curiousness scrunching her features while she studies the pack and the newcomers who fidget nervously. I imagine this isn't how they thought their first day here would go.

"Where the fuck are you taking us?" Kenna asks Bre, tugging her elbow from Bre's grip.

Instead of answering her, Bre opens the pantry door and lifts the oval rug off the floor. She throws the rug into the kitchen. It slides across the floor and thuds against the bottom cabinets under the sink. A hidden door lays where the rug once was, an entrance to the basement.

"Oh my," Darla breathes. "I didn't know that was there."

"We're really taking shelter?" Kenna asks. I hear the panic in her voice. She must not be a fan of storms. At least, the tornado-forming kind. By Irene's neutral expression, they don't frighten her, and if I were being honest with myself, they don't frighten me, either. Not a whole lot does these days.

Ben opens the heavy basement floor door and gestures for the pack to enter.

Jeremy turns while waiting to descend the stairs. "Is there an actual tornado on the ground?" he asks with mild curiosity, scratching at the stubble along his jaw.

The pack, including the new members, turns toward Evo while we wait for Kenna to waddle her way down with Bre. Kenna screeches from below, yelling something about giant, hairy, man-eating, eight-legged creatures. She must not be a fan of spiders, either, and I bite my lip to keep from grinning.

Kelsey peers down the steps and curses her agreement to Kenna's fear. "I'd rather chance the tornado," she grumbles.

"The radar indicates a tornado," Evo answers Jeremy. "That's all I know." He nods his head to the stairs, silently asking us to continue moving forward, eager to get to his pregnant mate.

Nodding, Jeremy steps down the first step after his mate. The new pack members file down next with Irene right behind them.

I watch her generous ass take each step. I watch too long to go unnoticed because Evo leans close to my ear and whispers with a hint of humor, "Are you going to follow or are you going to continue watching the show?"

I smirk a smug smile and follow Irene down, adjusting my pants against the strain of my growing erection with each step.

The basement is indeed full of cobwebs and a few stick to my cheek. There's not as many as one would think for not being down here for a while.

The tankless water heater is off to one side, while the rest of the space is lined with shelves that hold faded totes and aged boxes full of the pack's forgotten belongings and holiday decorations. I can feel the grit of dust under my shoes as I step onto the concrete floor, however, and sneeze as dust rises to my nose.

Irene walks to the far wall and sits down before a shelf, isolating herself from my pack. Or me. Either one is probable.

Distracting themselves from the wail of sirens and the push of wind outside, Kenna and Kelsey greet the new wolves as Bre introduces them one by one. Darla hovers beside Bre and hugs each of them tightly. Dyson stands off in a corner while Ben, Evo, and Jeremy huddle in their own private circle, discussing the weather and possible scenarios.

Thunder booms and rattles the house, and the women scream. Their screams frighten me, and my heart begins to pound loudly in my ears. My attention swivels to Irene who rests her chin against her knees pulled to her chest. She hadn't seemed bothered by the thunder like the rest.

Out of the corner of my eye, I watch as Dyson leans back into the corner, and crosses his arms over his chest.

Sighing, I make my way to him. Since there's no place to run and hide, I decide now is as good of a time as any to get this long overdue conversation out of the way.

At my approach, he picks a cobweb off his bare shoulder and props his foot against the wall behind him. I lean against the wall next to him, and together, watch the pack converse. "You've been avoiding me."

His bare shoulders bob with a shrug. "Not a whole lot to say."

Careful to not let my anger seep through my voice and alert the others, I murmur, "Want to tell me what the hell you were thinking?"

He adjusts his balance. "I was trying to keep you alive."

I snort and Evo looks in our direction with mild interest before returning to his conversation. "The safety of our alphas always comes first, Dyson." I turn my head and look at the side of his face. When was the last time he shaved? I continue, "The only ass you were saving was your own."

He drops his arms to his side and shifts his body to face mine. His eyebrows raise in disbelief, wrinkling his forehead. "Is that what you think? George would have killed you, Flint. Was I just supposed to sit by and watch that happen?"

Faceless people. Peppermint. Shouting. Pain. Flashes of that memory surface and I tick my jaw to the echoing pain of it. The lights in the basement flicker, but I barely notice. My wolf growls and paces inside me, disliking the flashback. "They were going to kill us anyway, you fool. You really think they would've handed us over in exchange for Kenna? You really think they would have held up their end of the bargain? If the pack hadn't stormed their territory, we would've been dead by morning."

His eyes narrow, but his shoulders rise and fall at a faster rate as his breathing quickens. "Excuse me for caring if you lived. Just remember, Flint, you're not the only one who suffers." He turns on his heel and strides to the adjacent wall. Noiselessly, he slides to the floor and rests his arms on his knees while glaring at his toes. An angry sneer is pasted on his face and he doesn't spare me another glance.

I stuff my hands into my pockets, thinking over his last words. I guarantee I suffered more than he did. He wasn't the one stuck inside his wolf, facing death.

Taking a few deep breaths, I study the scene around me. Like a magnet, my eyes land on my mate again and I visibly relax at her mere presence, content on memorizing her finest details. I watch as she picks at lint stuck to her jeans. She's a confident woman and danger, even of the

94

weather variety, doesn't seem to bother her. Kenna and Kelsey, however, have scooted so close to one another that they might as well be holding each other.

Irene's light brown skin is flawless, and each feature is symmetrical. She turns her face to the ladies chatting with the new pack members, but I can tell she isn't paying them any attention. Her ear is tilted in Ben, Evo, and Jeremy's direction, eavesdropping on their weather topics. I mentally add 'being informed' to my mate's capabilities and personality traits. It only makes me want her more.

Slowly, her head turns in my direction and her captivating eyes capture mine. My heart skips a beat, and my wolf takes notice. I blink slowly, keeping my eyes on her. She holds them for a moment, and it's enough for me to make a decision.

Striding over to her, I unhook my hands from my pant pockets and slide myself to the floor next to her. I give her points for not shifting away from me, even though the slight flare of her nostrils tells me she's dreading my presence. She's either deciding if she wants to sit by me or she's displeased with my company altogether. Maybe both. Probably both.

I bring my knees up and rest my elbows on them, mimicking her position. "How long do you plan to pretend I don't exist," I quietly ask her.

Without looking at me, she responds in the same hushed tone, "Long enough for you to realize I'm not interested."

I chuckle. "Could have fooled me." She fidgets uncomfortably and I smirk. "That's what I thought."

She whips her head to me. "Wipe that sexy smirk off your face. This may be news to you, but not everything is about you and what you desire, Flint Rockland."

I quirk an eyebrow at her angry gaze and challenge her to speak more – to get whatever is holding her back from me off her chest. She says nothing though, and it doesn't go unnoticed that this is the second time in minutes that I've been told I'm selfish. Perhaps I am, but I truly don't care. I am who I am, and mate or not, I refuse to change.

"Then why don't you explain it to me," I say, caressing this spitting kitten with a seductive tone.

She flings out an arm. "You really think this is the place to hold such a conversation?" The fight leaves her voice toward the end of the sentence. She's right, but I won't admit that out loud.

As we speak, the wind picks up volume, practically pushing through the small windows in the basement to curl around the room like invisible wraiths.

I let my arm brush against hers and instantly regret it. Shivering heat travels up my arm, to the pit of my stomach, and straight to my groin. I adjust myself, not caring if Irene witnesses the action.

"It's as good of a place as any . . . seeing as we're stuck here and all," I mumble. She shifts nervously again. I double blink, my eyelashes brushing my cheekbones. "You're nervous."

She frowns at me. "I'm not nervous."

"You are. But you're not nervous of the storm," I say, remember my earlier assessment. "Are you . . . do I make you nervous?" A half smile lifts my right cheek when she snorts unconvincingly. It's a cocky grin, and in this moment, I can't help but feel victorious.

She wipes the frown from her face and gives me a blank stare. "Do you want a cookie for your observation skills?"

I bark out with laughter, letting the back of my head drop against the shelf. That wasn't the response I was expecting. My laughter dies down and I clear my throat before speaking. "You can't run from me forever, Irene."

"I can try like hell."

"It's here," Evo announces to the room while glancing at the screen of his phone. The conversation dies down and everyone's attention shifts to Evo.

"What's here?" Kenna asks.

"A tornado," Ben answers.

Now, with silence in the room, I can truly hear the wind outside. It's louder than it should be. Like a train. I've always heard it described that way, but I never thought it would actually sound like one.

"Shit," I mumble, my legs dropping from their propped-up position.

For the first time, I see a moment of fear cross Irene's face. The house shakes and vibrates, and the room falls into complete darkness as the lights flicker off.

I grab Irene's shoulders and fold her top half inside my frame, covering her body with mine. I study the basement windows, and outside, all I can see is darkness and twigs pelting the windowpane. I don't spare a glance to the rest of my pack, concentrating only on Irene as I press my cheek into her spine. She whimpers in fright as something heavy hits the house. I shush her soothingly and rub her side while working like hell to restrain my wolf. I mentally shove my weight into the barrier inside me, desperate to keep him inside.

He's fearful, and again, wanting me to shift so he can flee. My body shakes as much as the house, but I use Irene's presence and scent to root me to my human shape. If I shift, I could hurt her. The fool doesn't realize there's nowhere for him to run even if he did have control.

The women scream as windows break somewhere inside the house. I squeeze Irene tighter, our breaths synced to each other's as it comes out in heavy, frightened huffs.

I don't know how long we huddled there. Seconds felt like minutes, but as the howling wind finally dies down, my heart rate slows. I uncurl myself from Irene and glance around the basement.

Jessup, Evalyn, Romaine, and Victoria huddle together in one corner while Ben, Evo, Kenna, Bre, and Darla are in another. Jeremy, Dyson, and Kelsey are gathered under the stairwell.

"Everyone okay?" Evo asks the group, peeking up from his mate's shoulder.

"Like fucking hell we are," Kenna spits at her mate. "That was a fucking tornado, wasn't it?" She moans and presses her hands to her tightening stomach.

Irene jumps from my lap and rushes over to Kenna's side. She examines Kenna's tightening belly with a concerned frown.

"Come on," Irene says, pulling Kenna up from the cement floor. She looks at Evo worriedly. "We need to get her upstairs."

*****

Jeremy whistles low as he, Ben, and I stand in the destruction of the backyard. The tornado never hit the house, but the damage outside is significant. At least the first few rows of trees are still standing, even if their leaves are gone and large branches dangle precariously toward the ground. Past that, trees are snapped in half from various heights of the trunks where the tornado had taken a clear path. Trunks, branches, and twigs are everywhere with chunks of hail, shingles, and the siding of the house peppered throughout.

The sirens can still be heard in the distance, but the threat for us has passed. The clouds no longer churn, and instead of downpouring, it only sprinkles as distant thunder rumbles the atmosphere.

Bre, Darla, Irene, and Evo are upstairs in the alphas' bedroom with Kenna, hovering over her. Before we left to check the damage, Irene said Kenna isn't in real labor, but she's subjected to resting the remainder of her pregnancy. She said something about high blood pressure. Kenna doesn't like it, but Irene told her if she didn't start taking care of herself, the baby would come early. The truth was enough to shut Kenna's mouth.

Miraculously, the SUV's parked out front survived the storm. The new wolves are unloading their belongings, while Kelsey is showing them to their quarters.

"What's the plan?" I ask Ben, bending to pick up a twig and examine the splintered, snapped end.

Ben places his hands on his hips and blows out a puff of air. "I guess we start by creating a pile to be burned." He pivots to me. "Feel like a bonfire tomorrow night?"

Still examining the twig, I ask, "You think the wood will be dry by then?"

"It's supposed to be hot tomorrow," Jeremy comments. "I bet it'll be dry by then."

Ben smiles impishly. "If not, we can always help it along."

I shrug, pretending indifference, when in reality, I'm glad he didn't mention a pack run to examine the forest's damage. I haven't shifted since I came back. I'm not ready for that yet, and my trust for the creature has yet to be regained.

I walk over to the first branch and throw it next to the large fire pit. It seems like a lifetime ago that we had used it. The last time we had a fire, a rogue wolf shot up the place. Dyson had been one of the wounded. I turn full circle to find the man in question, but he's nowhere to be seen. We were all told to come out here to start cleaning up.

"Where's Dyson?" I ask Ben who's staring at the other end of the spacious backyard and all the crap that litters across it. A pile of wood siding is in his arms.

He shrugs his shoulders and walks the short distance to drop his burden next to my branch. "Probably in his quarters."

I roll my eyes. The least he could do is give a hand. The more time that passes, the more I question what I saw in our friendship. We're nothing alike.

Or maybe we're no longer the same people.

I quickly shut down that thought and whistle a tune, going to the next branch and burying my troubles within my task.

Irene Scott

The door chimes as I step into the wiccan shop. The smell of incense reaches my sensitive nose, causing it to twitch.

A chipper Katriane smiles from behind the glass cashier counter. "Ira," she greets before dropping her smile and frowning. "Did you drive through that storm?"

Her dipped eyebrows distort her adorable pixie features. She's a beautiful woman, with a button

101

nose, large almond eyes, and a pitch black, pixie haircut.

Katriane Dupont, or Kat, is a witch from the Demi-Lune Coven. She had been the one who conducted a double unity service in the Cloven Pack territory. A unity service isn't necessary or the mating, but still, a witch must perform this sacred event.

A unity service ties a mated pair to the earth. Since witches often draw magic from the earth, wolf shifters and witches will sometimes work close together and keep close relationships. Nature is something we all have in common. Kat and I have a great friendship and I visit her shop often.

Kat owns this shop, Lunaire, where she sells wiccan trinkets, books, and herbal remedies. Most of her witch-related inventory is fake for obvious reasons. The shop is located in a tourist area of the city and the last thing anybody wants is for a human to come into contact with anything magical.

In the back of the shop, through the closed door at the end of the hall, is where the real magic lies. Behind that closed door are some seriously witchy things.

Though Kat is a petite little thing, she can hold her own. Unlike most witches, she's outspoken, has a great sense of morals and justice, and she's the black sheep—as in, she doesn't dress the part. Most witches are conservative. They refuse to draw attention to themselves. Kat, on the other hand, likes to dress in black and tattoos cover much of her skin. There's more to this girl than meets the eye, that much I'm sure of.

Witches usually live in a house or on a property together with elaborate stories on why there's so many women under one roof. They live similarly to the way packs do, except they don't shift into another form. Their covens are generally small because they keep their numbers low. It's a purposeful act. Secrecy is more important to them than it is to us. They've been sacrificed more throughout history than shifters have.

And though there are some similarities between wiccan and shifter lifestyles, the DNA part of things is completely different. The witch's magical trait is passed down by DNA, just like shifters, but with one exception: witches are always women. There's never been a single male witch born, a fact that I find completely interesting.

Crossing the shop, I pick up a tiny statue of their crescent placed next to the register. Heavy and about the size of my hand, I take note of the smooth surface of the half-moon with a strike through it. It's such a simple symbol, but I find it interesting how ironic it is. Wolf shifters are thought to be the supernatural creatures who are held by the moon and here's a witch coven, and a dear friend of mine, whose crest is a half-moon.

"Well, actually, I was sort of in it," I comment distractedly, still lost in my own thoughts.

"Like, 'in it,' in it?"

I glance up at her. Her little brows are still furrowed. "Sure was. I'm staying with the Cloven Pack, because their alpha female is pregnant. The tornado went through their forest." I set the statue back on the counter and rest my elbows on the glass surface.

Kat's face lights up with acknowledgment. "Oh yes, I've heard about this. This is the alpha female in the double unity, isn't it?" I nod confirmation. "Isn't she a Queen Alpha or whatever?" I nod again. "I hear she can be a real bitch."

I laugh at her outspoken truth. "She can, yes. But I think it has more to do with her upbringing. I'm told it wasn't a pleasant one." I rub my thumb over the half moon. "She's actually a nice girl, but she hides it behind her words."

Kat twists her lips to the side, considering this information. "Makes sense, I suppose. So, what brings you by today?"

I stand up straight. "Kenna has preeclampsia and some strong Braxton Hicks. I was hoping you'd have something to help with her blood pressure."

Kat holds up a finger, walks around the counter, and heads toward the rack of herbs. While she searches, I strike up conversation. "How's the coven?" I ask.

She keeps her back to me as she replies, "There was a virus spreading through the coven . . ." She grabs a little bottle of dried herbs and walks around the back of the counter. "My mom and I aren't getting along because I broke a few rules to cure them."

"Oh?" I press, leaning into the glass of the counter.

"Yeah." She quickly changes the subject, flipping the conversation back to me. "What about you? How are you liking the Cloven Pack?"

I clear my throat. *I've found my mate, I want to 'get hitched,' but unfortunately, that scenario isn't in the cards for me.* But I don't tell her any of those things. No way do I want to have that discussion with someone who doesn't believe in mates. Witches aren't allowed to fall in love. They're not allowed to marry, either. I've never asked Kat where she stands on that rule, even though she breaks all the others. So, instead, I say, "It's a nice pack. Much smaller than the Riva Pack and very close-knit."

She nods and rings me up. "What are you doing tomorrow night? Want to hang out?"

I check the total on the small screen and hand her the cash. "Actually, we're having a bonfire to burn up all the debris. If you want, you can come along," I suggest with a shrug.

Kat nods again and places my purchased herbs in a small bag. "Sounds like a riot. I've never been to a shifter party before."

I smile at her. "Good. I'll see you tomorrow, then."

I grab my sack and head toward the door, waving as I exit. Though wet with fresh rain, the pavement radiates heat up my exposed calves. I walk back to my car at the side of the shop and fish for my keys inside my small purse. Pressing the unlock button, I hop inside my car and distractedly insert the key into the ignition.

Driving through the rest of town, I pull onto the quiet blacktop and continue my way back to the Cloven Pack territory.

Irene? my alpha, Jacob, asks telepathically.

His voice in my head was so abrupt, that the car swerved. *Jacob? Are you okay?*

Yes, we're fine. We got the tail end of the storm. I just saw on the news—was the Cloven Pack hit with a tornado?

I sigh in relief. *Yes, we –* I mentally stumble in my speech *– they were.* I remind myself that this isn't my pack. After a moment of silence, I continue, *No one was hurt and there wasn't much damage done to the house. A thinning of the woods is the most of it.*

I can hear the relief in his next words. *That's good. Call me if the pack needs help cleaning the mess.*

I'm about to respond when my attention is pulled to the cars reflecting in my rearview mirror. This road is never busy. I frown as a black SUV drives in the wrong lane, speeds past me, and slams on its brakes.

My lungs seize in my chest. I slam my foot down on the brake pedal and my car screeches to a halt. My wolf growls inside me, furious and frightened.

"What the fuck?" I shout, banging my hand on the horn. I look out all my windows as more cars arrive and box me in. There's one car in front—the asshole who slammed on his brakes—one in the opposite lane beside me, and one car at the rear.

I slump back in my seat, knowing that I'm not going anywhere.

The SUV's door opens, and I groan when I recognize the face as he heads in my direction. Zane flicks the end of his cigarette onto the road. Embers bounce along the pavement until they spark out of life.

"What now, Zane?" I mumble to myself. Unbuckling my seatbelt, I unlock my doors. There's no sense in trying to keep him out—he'll just break the glass. Rogue wolves have no quarrels with such things, I've learned.

I roll down my window instead of climbing out of the car. I don't want to exit unless it's necessary. Last time, I was nearly tackled to the ground.

He approaches my window and peers inside. No doubt, he's checking for weapons.

Satisfied, he leans back and says in an emotionless tone, "Get out of the car."

"No."

"Out," he barks. "Now."

I blink at him and sigh, resigning to my fate.

Exiting the car, I turn my attention to Luke as he giggles hysterically. His clothes are, yet again, soiled in grease, with slimy blond hair to match. His blackened teeth make me cringe as he shoots me one more smile. He passes a black cloth to Zane, and then hops in my car. My teeth grind as he turns on my radio, pressing a button to switch from my jazz station. Rock music blares through my speakers.

"Let's get this show on the road," Luke hoots over the music, drumming his hands on the steering wheel.

I glance at the black cloth in Zane's hand. Void of words and emotion, he places it over my head and my world goes dark. Only sounds guide me as he shoves me into his SUV.

CHAPTER EIGHT

Flint Rockland

Kenna throws her hands into the air. "Will you guys stop the chit-chat?" she asks. "You're making the baby excited, which makes him," she pauses with a frown, "or her sucker-punch my kidneys." She winces in pain and her hands fly to her swollen stomach.

Evo and Kenna had decided not to find out the gender. Something about wanting it to be a surprise. I don't like surprises—I'd rather know what I'm in for, but thankfully, this isn't my child and it's not my opinion that matters.

Kenna, sitting next to me on the couch, sighs when the chatter hushes to a more endurable volume. Next to her, Evo stands from his seat and moves to the front of the living room, effectively blocking the TV that displays the news. The news is showing the damage from the storm and all anyone seems to be talking about is the tornado. It's understandable, but we have more important things to worry about.

Bre, laying on the floor with her head in Ben's lap, turns to Kenna. "Where's Irene?" she asks.

"She said something about a spice shop? Or a witch hunt?" She sighs, closes her eyes, and rubs the space between her eyebrows. "Fucking hell, I can't remember which."

A slow smile creeps across Bre's face and I do my best not to laugh. Kenna, feeling my emotions without even having to look at me, hits me in the chest before the laughter can escape.

God, it feels good to have joy. I haven't found much of it lately. The feeling spreads warmth to areas that have been drowning in darkness. It's exhilarating—a close second to an adrenaline rush.

I'd been wondering where Irene was, but I didn't want to voice it aloud. I had figured she was in her room, not feeling the need to be in on a pack meeting when she isn't a pack member. She could be, if she wanted to. An idiot could see how much she loves it here. All she has to do is let me in – accept me as her mate.

Evo's snarl vibrates the room, and we again quiet our chatter, sheepish looks on our faces.

"Alright, so everyone has met the new members, yes?" The room's heads bob as one. "Good, then we'll skip the introductions. With the damage from the tornado, we'll have an abundance of wood to burn. Tomorrow night, we'll have a bonfire to get rid of all the debris."

Darla crosses her legs, pride in her posture. "Kelsey and I have already mapped out the meal."

Evo's teeth grind, his ears flexing with the movement for being interrupted again, but he nods anyway.

Before he can continue, Victoria leans toward Darla. "I can help with that, too, Mrs. Kenner."

"Oh, darling. Please call me Darla. I'm no longer mated, and besides, Mrs. Kenner makes me sound old."

On the chair to the left of where Evo stands, Romaine's broad shoulders push forward as he leans his elbows against his knees. "Was there any more damage aside from the trees?"

My eyes land on Dyson when he looks at Kelsey. "What are we having?" he asks her disinterestedly. He hasn't been talking . . . or participating for that matter, in any group settings, so why would he care? I study him from head to toe. His clothes are wrinkled, there's crumbs on his shirt, and stubble has surfaced across his jaw. His hair is a mess and he has dark circles under his eyes.

I chew on the inside of my lip as guilt surfaces inside me. Maybe he's right. Maybe I'm not the only one who's trying to deal with the cards they've been dealt. Too busy holding a grudge, I haven't given Dyson the time of day since my wolf let me shift.

Evo answers Romaine, "No. So far all the damage is secluded to the woods." He turns back to the room, his whistle bouncing off the walls and vibrating my eardrums. Kenna and Bre cover their ears while Ben holds back a smile and glances at me. Seems like adding new members to the pack is going to be a bit of an adjustment to our once small and manageable numbers.

"Now that I have your attention," he growls, "what's this about missing Gray Pack members?"

Ben walks Evo through everything we've learned, from the wolves sneaking off in the night, to the empty safe. I watch as Evo's face twists in anger at certain points in the recap. He tries his best to hide his feelings on the matter, but he's failing miserably.

Kenna, uncomfortable with her mate's rising emotions, shifts in her cushion. I put my arm around her and let her lean against me while we listen to our alpha and beta's discussion.

Evo Johnson

I sit down heavily in my office chair, a huff of air leaving the cushioned leather seat. Today has been exhausting. If it's not one thing, it's another. The only good thing about today is that this morning, I felt the baby kick my cheek when I pressed my face against Kenna's belly.

Ben enters my office and I gesture for him to sit in his usual chair in front of me. He takes a seat, searching my eyes. "Are you thinking what I'm thinking?" he asks.

I shrug. "Who's our only enemy left? We already know she was conspiring with George Kenner, and she was mates with Chris Kenner. It stands to reason . . ."

"She might have some of the Gray wolves on her side." He rests his elbows on his knees and nods. "She would most likely know about the safe if that's the case."

"Every pack has a safe like that. It's where we keep our valuables . . . and our pack member papers." Whoever stole it didn't want us to know who had gone rogue. I scratch my chin, bits and pieces of this aren't fitting together. "How'd she open the safe?"

"Oh, I doubt she was there at all," Ben says. "We would have scented her. Besides, Victoria knew the safe's code. She couldn't have been the only one who did." Ben scrubs his face and leans back in his chair, defeated from today's events, just as me. "The new wolves seem to be fitting in nicely."

I pick up a pen and twirl it in my fingers, eager for a switch of subject. "Yeah? All moved in?"

Ben nods before we both get lost in our thoughts. The pen continues to twirl in my fingers until it clinks on my wooden desk and drops to the carpet. I don't bother picking it up. Not this time.

The sound breaks Ben's silence. "Why would they go to Jazz? And why disappear without a word?"

I frown. "Maybe we should send out a search party."

"For who? Jazz or the missing wolves? If we don't have their papers, we won't know who to look for."

Shrugging, I turn down my lips for a moment. "Both. We have to try. You and I both know that they're with her. There's too many coincidences to believe otherwise."

He shakes his head. "A lot of hell that'll do. We wouldn't know where to start looking. Even if we got the names from our new members . . ."

I rub my eyebrow, placing as much pressure as I can into the twitching muscle. "Yeah."

Ben scratches his head. "The whole thing pisses me off."

The skin on the back of my arms squeak against the leather as I lift them in a shrug. "There's nothing we can do about it now. But Ben? Let's keep this information to ourselves for now. I don't want to alarm Kenna that Jazz may have an army of shifters."

Ben nods, his eyes downcast.

Irene Scott

Zane opens the side door of the SUV and grabs my arm.

"I can do it, damn it," I bark. He drops his hand and growls at my outburst.

Blindfolded, and with my hands tied, I carefully shimmy to the side of the seat and place my feet on the familiar gravel driveway. The sun beats on my skin as I stand upright after exiting the car. My head shifts left and right, though I can't see anything. It's

114

an automatic response to try and absorb my surroundings.

The chirping birds and the trees rustling in the wind are my only background noise. Ending his growl, Zane rips the black bag from my head, taking strands of my hair with it. I yelp in surprise, not expecting such abrupt pain.

I squint my eyes and adjust to the light. Everything is exactly as I remembered from my visit during the winter, except now, little critters scurry about within the unkempt green grass surrounding the large shed. I still can't figure out why they call it 'The Castle.'

Yanking me along, Zane lumbers a path to the shed as the other cars pull in and park behind the SUV.

The large metal doors open for us and we step inside to the surprisingly cool temperature of the shed's interior. My eyes take a moment to adjust to the darkness, though, and a headache forms behind them from the constant changes in lighting.

Chatter dies down and I glance to my left. Around the dining table, the rogues are having an early meal. My stomach growls at the smell of their food, but I ignore it. I've heard the rumors about what rogues like to eat, and I'd rather not find out if the gossip rings true.

Jazz, seated at the head of the table, dabs her mouth with a white cloth napkin. "Irene," she says, and then takes a sip of a red wine. I can smell its sweet aroma from where I stand.

I rip my arm from Zane's grasp as the other wolves trickle in behind us. They close the door. "Jazz– er– The One," I counter, clearing my throat. "I mean – Do I bow?"

Her expression remains blank and she ignores my question. I shift my feet, uncomfortable with this situation and the rising tension that stretches between us. My wolf whines inside of me. She doesn't like being closed in and surrounded by enemies.

Jazz scoots out her chair and stands with her hands, palms flat, against the table. "I thought we had a deal, Irene."

My eyes search the other wolves around the dining table, nervousness making my muscles coil. I flick my gaze down the hallway to where I know my brother is being held. "Yes. I remember the deal."

A small smile lifts the corners of her lips and it's anything but kind. "Good. Is there a reason why I haven't heard from you in months?"

I clear my throat and shift away from Zane who looks ready to pounce at any given command. "I've, ah . . . I've been busy. And I wasn't sure how to contact you."

Jazz glances around at her wolves. They've shifted their attention back to her, curious and eager for her next move or response.

"Is my brother okay?" I ask. "Are you feeding him? I want to see him."

"Your brother is fine." Her tone slithers in a way that reminds me of a snake. "He's taking a little nap right now." When she pinches her pointer finger and thumb together as a gesture to the word 'small,' rage builds inside me. The rogues laugh and my suspicions are confirmed.

"What'd you do to him?" I ask, my posture defensive as I growl at her. My eyes glow green and Zane grips my upper arm. His firm grasp, fingers digging into my skin, snaps me back to reality and the real dangers that losing my shit could pose.

Jazz's face is the picture of innocence as she places her hand over her heart. "I didn't do anything." At this moment, I wish I had Kenna's gift so I could effectively call her out on her bullshit. Little good it would do me, though. I'd still be severely outnumbered, and I doubt the rogues would care if she's lying or not.

She walks around the table and stands in front of me. Her perfume wafts across my face like heavy smoke. "We had a deal, Miss Scott. So far, you haven't lived up to your end." She bats her long, fake eyelashes. The glitter in her eyeshadow shimmers persistently while I fight the urge to move away. "I don't give favors to those who don't deliver on their promises. Now, do you have any information for me?"

I chew on the inside of my lip, my heart torn. How can I choose? Save my brother or save the pack and the mate I barely know. There's no right answer. There's no easy way to get out of this mess. *Please, forgive me*, I plea inside my head. "No. There's nothing to report."

Luke giggles behind me. "Can we torture it out of her?"

I fight against Zane's grip, but he's much stronger than I am. He wraps me in a bear hug, my back to his chest, and curls his arm around my neck. I stand on my tiptoes to keep breathing, the blood rushing to my face, and wait for Jazz's verdict.

She taps her chin before giving her final answer. "No. I have a new proposition." She places her hands behind her back. "Clearly, you don't plan to give up the Cloven Pack alphas. My new proposal . . ." she holds up a finger before I can ask, "I want you to bring the baby to me."

My eyes bulge. *Bring the baby* . . . "No." My answer is firm, final, and not up for discussion.

She smiles sickly sweet. "You know, Irene, you're not the only spy we have. You are . . ." she pauses, twisting her lips to the side, "disposable."

I struggle within Zane's arms again, kicking my feet in every direction. He snaps his teeth next to my ear and I stiffen. "Then why the hell do you need me?" I bark.

"Because I get what I want." She laughs and her rogue entourage joins in. "Who would suspect the Cloven Pack midwife as a traitor?"

Flint Rockland

Wiping the sweat from my forehead with a towel, Ben slaps me on the back for a job well done. A slight sting remains where his hand hit my wet skin. We had just completed another session in the gym. If my sore muscles are anything to go by, he never once held back. I'm grateful for that fact, and his ability to take my mind off of everything.

"Outside, everyone," Ben says, ushering the pack from their machines and out the door for our daily sparring sessions.

As the last one out of the gym, I flick off the lights, close the door, and step into the chilly morning air. The slight breeze caresses my hot skin, drying the sweat and raising goosebumps.

Kenna, basking in the morning light, sips from a mug. Her large protruding belly pushes out past the arm rests of the chair. To her displeasure, she's not allowed to have caffeine, but luckily, Darla bought her decaf when she got sick of her daughter's whining. She's lucky anyone allowed her out here. Irene had given her strict instructions to stay in bed.

She and Darla are the only ones excluded from sparring, Kenna from the obvious reasons, and Darla being the one who volunteered to cook breakfast. More like she beat Kelsey to volunteering . . . much to Kelsey's dismay. I've gathered that Darla doesn't involve herself with violence, even when it's to learn how to protect herself.

"Partner up," Ben hollers. "Jeremy and Jessup. Bre and Victoria. Evo and Romaine. Flint and Dyson." He continues, but I don't listen.

Whipping my head around, I glance at a Dyson. His eyebrows knit together, his jaw ticking as he refuses to meet my gaze.

I tip my head to the side. Why would Ben pair us together?

When he's done calling off names, the pack disperses into their pairs and confine themselves to separate areas on the lawn.

I stay where I am, dumbfounded.

This isn't a punishment, Flint. Talk to him, Evo says telepathically. I narrow my eyes at my alpha's back as he walks past me and heads toward Romaine.

Begrudgingly, I crunch through the fresh grass and stand in front of Dyson. He sighs, understanding that he won't be getting out of this either, and assumes his fighting position.

Halfheartedly, I do the same before the sparring begins. He throws his fist at me. There's no effort whatsoever behind the action. I dodge my head, avoiding it easily, my eyes squinting in annoyance.

I thrust my hand forward and connect with his jaw. His head snaps to the side and he slowly turns his head back to me, finally looking me in the eyes. I observe him quickly, taking in the protruding cheekbones and the faint purple circles under his eyes. He looks like he hasn't eaten or slept in days.

His jaw ticks again, his eyes steel, and he picks up his sparring's pace, fueled by the hit.

We get moving, our bodies sweating, his face softening as we fall into a rhythm like old times. It isn't long before I break the silence. "Do you still dream about it?"

Without missing a beat, he answers with a grunt, "Yes."

I wait for a few punches to be swapped before I ask my next question. "Do you get any sleep?"

His fist lands on my stomach and a slight oof comes from my mouth. "Not a whole lot, no."

"Do you feel guilty?"

He steps back during my next punch and my fist swings through the empty air. He stares at me, his jaw ticking again, and his expression returns to hardened steel once more. Dyson can't conceal all of his emotions, however. Some of his emotions subtly tick across the muscles of his face, but they're too fleeting. I can't read them as they flit on by. His pain is evident, though.

"Yes," he finally mumbles.

Turning to leave, he walks back to his quarters without another word. I watch his retreating back until he slips through his door and closes it softly behind him.

A tiny bit of the wall I've built for avoiding Dyson falls. A wave of my own emotions flood through me, attempting to drown me. I've been a bit intense lately, but I'm not an emotionless bastard. I see him hurting, and the friend that I used to be wants to fix it. But how can I fix it if I'm no longer that same person? If he's no longer the same person? I don't know this Flint—I'm still getting used to the changes in my personality. So, it begs for consideration: Who is Dyson now?

I sigh, resolved to having no answers, and glance around. Most of the sparring partners are done and heading to the alpha quarters for our meal. The grass where the partners had spared is flattened to the dirt, and birds cross the cloudy sky.

Jeremy walks up to me and slaps me on the back. "We'll see you in a few weeks. Try not to destroy the place without me."

I frown at him. "What do you mean? Where are you going?"

Confusion pulls his eyebrows together. "No one told you?" I shake my head. "Kelsey and I are leaving today. We're going south for our mating anniversary."

"Oh," I mumble. For a moment, I feel disconnected from my pack. I've missed so much. Time was stolen from me – time I'll never get back. I wipe my self-pity away and paste a smile on my face. "Enjoy, then." I point at him. "Keep her away from the margaritas."

He holds up a hand and closes his eyes. "You don't have to tell me twice."

I give him a nod. He strides to his mate, gathers her in his arms, and together, they take off to their quarters.

I glance up at Kenna on the back porch. She's sitting next to Irene. I hadn't noticed Irene's return from wherever she like to wander off to, but now, the breeze carries her scent to me.

Irene meets my gaze, and my feet move before I tell them to. I quickly climb the steps while she finishes her sentence to Kenna. I don't know what they were talking about, but, as if she didn't see my approach, she stands from the chair and enters the house through the sliding glass door, effectively running from me . . . *again*.

Huffing, I follow after her. She can't keep running from me. I won't let her.

I see her turn the corner and climb the stairs toward her guest bedroom. The sound of her soft footfalls are smothered by the loud and joyous conversation happening inside the kitchen. A tiny growl escapes my lips and I quicken my pace to a jog across the dining room.

I finally catch up with her in the upstairs hallway. "Irene," I call out. "Irene, wait a minute."

She stops on the hallway rug, her body rigid. "What?" she asks without turning around.

Double blinking, I work to ignore the panging ache in my chest to her displeasure at my request. I pause before walking around to the front of her. Still, she keeps her eyes on the floor, so I bend my knees to capture her gaze. Her brown irises settle on mine.

"Can we talk?" I ask.

She slides her hands in her jean pockets. "About?"

I laugh without humor and shake my head. "When are you going to stop pretending?"

"Pretending what?" Her tone is flat and it doesn't settle well with me.

I visually trace every feature of her face. "You're hiding from me. I'll figure out why, I always do. But you can't keep running from your mate." I reach and tuck a stray hair behind her ear, my skin briefly touching hers. She closes her eyes and inhales my scent as I do the same. It fills my heart again, chases away that *ache*, and I try like hell to seal it inside. It's a craving, an addiction, and I'll never get enough.

"I'm not ready to be mates," she answers honestly. She opens her eyes. For a moment, I get lost in their brown depths—swirls of yellow mingle with the brown, distracting me from my train of thought. I clear my throat, but she's not finished. "Look, I'm normally not this cold. I don't have a black heart. I just know nothing about you, and I have my own crap going on. Just because we're mates doesn't mean I plan to jump into any relationship."

I nod, respecting her answer and coming up with a simple solution. "Go on a date with me, then."

Her eyes widen, her expression taken aback. "Like . . . a date, date?"

With a smug smile, I take a step closer to her, invading her personal space and using the lure of mate vs mate to sway her answer in my favor. "Yes, a real date." I brush my fingertips against her cheek, feeling the soft, warm skin under them. How is it possible for someone to be so soft – so smooth? My eyes search hers, pleading for the chance. "Say yes. Please, say yes."

She waits for a moment, agonizingly weighing her options. Her bottom lip sucks into her mouth and she subtly bites down. My heart sings when she nods. It sings and sails over mountains and across dark seas.

I grin. Gently, I tug her bottom lip free with my thumb. Her soft exhale doesn't go unnoticed.

Jasmyn Schueler

I sit on my throne, the queen of my castle. My loves gather around me, some standing, some sitting on the couches. Through my guidance, everything I see before me, I've provided for them. I give them what they desire most. How could they not adore me?

"The One," Zane addresses me, squatting to catch my wandering gaze. "What do you want to do?"

I search the eyes of my subjects. They seek my guidance, and I must do them no wrong. I must prove my strength and gain vengeance for my beloved. With them, I can rule over more than just these wolves.

"Call our spy and get ahold of *them*," I say. "And Zane, take Luke with you. Do the job close to their territory. We don't need their alpha feeling the pack

125

link break before our plan unfolds. We need them all in one place. We need them distracted."

I stroke the brown hair of the female sitting on the floor below me. What's her name? I don't remember. It's unimportant. She means little to what I have to gain. "Come tomorrow, I suspect the Cloven Pack will be paying a little visit . . . after they've mourned." I peck the lips of the adorning female and give her a loving smile that doesn't reach my heart. My heart has been long dead, and I have no plans to revive it. Emotions are for fools.

Flint Rockland

I place my hand on the lower part of her back and guide her through the restaurant doors. The place is dim with romantic candles lit on every table, and soft instrumental music plays in the background. It should be perfect for winning her affections. That's the plan, anyway, but these days, my plans don't always work in my favor.

Irene seems to be rebelling against the very idea of sharing a meal with me. The whole way here she sat stiffly in the passenger seat and stared out the window. I don't think she hates me in particular, but instead, the idea of a mate. I don't understand it, but I will get to the bottom of it.

At least she let me drive. In fact, she demanded it, saying that there was a foul smell inside her car.

A host takes us to our reserved table, and I pull the chair out for Irene. She smiles a little, and with a soft sigh, she sits as I scoot the chair toward the table.

One point for Flint, I mentally award.

I take my seat and hand her a black menu. Her hands shake as she grasps the edge and pulls it to her. She's nervous. I have to admit, so am I. I have one shot here — one chance to show her that I'm worth having a meal with.

I lean across the small, round table. "You know, I don't bite. Well, maybe a little." I wink.

She stares at me, completely uninterested in my attempts at seduction. "Do you say that to all the ladies or just the ones you're trying to bed?"

My smile grows wider. My dick springs to life, straining against the inside of my slacks. I switch the subject, hoping to stave off the uncomfortable erection. Perhaps seduction isn't the best approach. "Have you been here before?" I glance at my menu and pretend to read it. I've been here plenty of times to know my favorites, but it provides a distraction from her intense gaze.

"I have," she says while readjusting her silverware.

I look over the top of my menu, curiosity getting the better of me when she says nothing else. "Really? With who?"

Her eyes travel across the menu's items. "A date," she provides.

My blood boils with jealousy, my mood souring. My heart beats rapidly, and for a moment, I can hear my blood thumping in my ears. My wolf growls inside me, but I move my thoughts away from hunting down this male and strangling him with my bare hands, to something . . . lighter. Like bunnies . . . hopping through a forest . . . their dusty tails poking above the grass . . . their triangle noses twitching as fast as my pounding heart.

Nope. Not working.

She glances up from her menu when I don't respond and sees me struggling. Placing the menu down, she folds her hands across the top of it. "You know, I'm not an idiot. I've heard the rumors. How do you think I feel knowing you've taken dozens of other women to your bed?"

My posture stiffens further and the blood drains from my face before I consider her question. My shoulders relax, realization dawning on me that I may not be the only one struggling with jealousy. I stretch my neck, rolling out the kinks, and pick back up the menu. "Fair point," I grumble. Another switch of subject. *Think, Flint. Think.* "Have you had the roasted duck? It's pretty good." She shakes her head. "Good. Let's get that and a bottle of white wine?"

I wait for her to disagree, but she lifts her glass of water and sips daintily while she discreetly studies the room. I watch her throat, compelled by the way it moves when it forces the water down. My dick twitches, straining against my clothes again as I envision other, more interesting things, being swallowed. I adjust my pants, moving the zipper to the left.

Taking her lack of response as the go-ahead, I wave the waitress over and place our order.

The waitress lingers, but I turn my attention back to the beauty in front of me, ignoring the flaunting of cleavage the waitress practically waves in my face as she takes my menu. "Do you have any family?" I ask Irene.

The waitress gets the hint, huffs, and moves away from our table.

Irene frowns at the waitress who's returning the menus to the hostess's booth. Out of the corner of my eye, I see her leaning to gossip with the hostess, and together, they both peek over their shoulders at me. "Yes," Irene finally says. "My parents are dead, but I have one brother."

I nod my head, relieved to have her full attention once more. "Is he living at the Riva Pack?"

She clears her throat and toys with her napkin. I note her reluctance before she answers. "No. He, ah . . . he moved after he got back from the war. I haven't talked to him in years." Her refusal to make eye contact causes me to frown. She straightens out her napkin. With her tone lighter, more chipper, she asks, "What about you? Any family?"

The frown still on my face, I answer, "No. Well, yes. But I haven't seen or heard from my parents in years."

"I'm sorry," she says sincerely.

I shrug and take a sip of water, uncomfortable with her sympathy. "It's no big deal. We're better off a part."

The waitress returns with our wine and fills our glasses. I keep my eyes on Irene as she watches the white liquid lick the inside of her wine glass. Her sensual lips are a shade darker than her skin, and they twitch in anticipation of the first sip.

Another waiter brings out a silver platter with a lid. Surprise lights her features when the waiter lifts the lid and reveals the roasted duck within. She glances at me and I can't help but grin. He sets it between us while a bowl of salad is placed next to it. Then, he bows and leaves without uttering a single word.

Irene's tongue licks her bottom lip, and for some odd reason, her briefly visible tongue is all I can pay attention to. I adjust my pants once more and take a deep breath to push aside what she does to me.

She snaps her napkin open and drapes it across her lap. "That was fast. When you said we were having duck, I thought we'd be here for a while."

"It's their specialty tonight." My voice is gruffer than I mean it to be. "They always have them ready to serve."

Nodding, she picks up her fork and begins to assemble her plate. The aroma of the meal drifts to my nose while I watch her every move.

"I heard this place is hard to get into," she mutters.

"It is," I admit as she hands me the salad bowl.

She pauses her fork midway to her mouth. "Do you know someone here or something?"

"I do." Pulling food onto my own plate, I take a bite of the duck. An explosion of flavors travel over my tongue. I point to my mouth. "You should try this. It's amazing."

Raising a brow, she does as I suggest. Her lips close over the meat skewered on her fork. Her eyelids close, and she hums. The makeup on her eyelids shimmer in the dim lighting, a taunting tease that dares me to reach across and touch her, taste her, hear her moan for reasons unrelated to the food. My mouth dries and my throat constructs.

Shit.

"This is amazing," she whispers, and then considers me thoughtfully. "You know a lot of people, don't you." It wasn't a question. The assumption popped out of her mouth without a second thought. Her gaze travels around my face, and her expression softens like she's truly seeing me for the first time. She double blinks, realizing how brash her comment was. "Not that that's a bad thing. I'm not a gold digger. I don't care how many people you know and who you know. I –" Her hand trembles as she touches her forehead and rubs at her eyebrow. "It was just an observation. I didn't mean to imply—"

I place my hand atop hers. Sizzling, electric heat travels through the contact and she stiffens to the sensation. Wide, brown eyes swivel up to mine and her shoulders rise and fall as her breath quickens.

"I know what you meant," I murmur. I reluctantly take back my hand and return to eating. My stomach twists and turns with nervous energy. "You going to eat?" I ask after a moment of holding eye contact, pretending indifference to the effect she has on me. At least I know this isn't a one-way street. At least I know she can't deny the attraction, because I can certainly scent it in the air.

Irene Scott

I should have never agreed to this.

I shift in the passenger seat, the car's leather squeaking with my movement. The way this guy makes me feel . . . Every sensitive part of me is swollen, throbbing, and begging for attention.

I try to focus out the car window, but it's dark and there isn't much to see. I turn my eyes back to the inside of Flint's car and observe all the button's soft lights. I suppose it's the pack's car and not necessarily his, but the interior is nice, clean, and there's a faint smell of leather polish.

Nervous, and my hands fidgeting because of it, I reach for the radio button at the same time Flint does. Our hands touch and I automatically pull mine back. He looks at me, an eyebrow raised, and then presses the button. Soft jazz plays through the speakers, filling the car with a slow and beautiful musical piece.

Switching his attention between the road and me, he exhales softly, plucks my hand from my lap, and folds it in his. His hands are large and calloused, and his thumb rubs slow circles on the back of my hand. My heart thuds impossibly fast and butterflies flutter about in my stomach. I debate about taking my hand back, but . . . the sensation he creates is the sort of anticipation that I couldn't ignore even if I wanted to. Anticipation for what could be. Anticipation for what might come.

Involuntarily, my mind goes straight to the gutter. Images of what his fingers could do jump through my mind. I squeeze my legs shut against the throbbing ache between my thighs and try my best to control my breathing.

Flint's lips turn up into a sly smile. "Does this affect you, Ira?"

I clear my throat, my mouth dry. "Is sex all you think about?" I ask weakly.

His eyebrows lower but the sly smile continues. "Get to know me and find out for yourself."

I clench my jaw to the way his voice, deep and rumbling, sounds. He chuckles, understanding I'm stubborn enough not to admit what he does to me. "Is it always this intense with mates?" The question popped out before I could consider it and how he might take it. I can feel my resolve lower, feel my stubbornness at denying my mate evaporate with each passing second we're together.

He doesn't answer me, but a smoldering heat charges the car's atmosphere. "What if I slid my fingers inside you? What if I pumped them in and out? Watched you squirm? Listened to you calling my name? But I won't let you come, not until I say so—not until you beg . . ."

Sweat builds along my spine and my thighs visibly quiver. His arousal stuffs its way up my nose and my nipples pebble in response. His fingers clench the wheel tighter.

Normally, I wouldn't like such dirty talk. Normally, I would have slapped any man who talked to me that way. But coming from my mate . . . His words have power. How am I supposed to ignore this? The pull is so strong, our arousals so evident, only a fool would be oblivious.

He pulls into the gravel driveway and slows his speed as the car nears the garage. The pack house's lights shine across the hood of the car. Pressing the button to open the large garage door, he then eases the car inside. The way he parks it accentuates the stretched and tight silence.

I wet my lips, accidentally tasting his desire lingering about the small space.

The garage door closes behind us and we're left staring at each other in the dark. His eyes glow wolf, taking on the green hue. I'm sure mine are doing the same, and soon, the green casts shadows along the dashboard.

He opens the car door and climbs out. His soft footsteps can be heard above my heavy breaths as he strides with purpose to my side of the car and opens my door.

Placing my palm in his outstretched hand, I let him aid me out of the car. He shuts the door and steps closer to me. His nearness – his invasion of my space – makes my heart thud in my ears.

Automatically, I visually trace his lips. Even in the darkness they shine, smooth and inviting. I step back, bumping into the side of the car. He matches my step and presses his body lightly against mine. The rigid muscles of his chest push against my breasts, and the heat coursing off him chases away the chill of the garage.

My gaze travels up, my night vision having no difficulty seeing every detail of his face. His lips are slightly parted and his breath, sluggishly leaving his mouth, fans my burning cheeks.

Carefully, he tucks a stray hair behind my ear, then brushes the back of his knuckles down the side of my neck. I shiver.

My trembling hands find their way to his hips and my fingertips take in the heat of his body. He takes my touch as a gesture to continue his advance. My head tells me this is a bad idea, but my heart begs me to let this play out – to see where it goes.

He places his free hand on the small of my back while the other curves around my jaw. I lean into it and my eyelids flutter shut for a moment while I dwell peacefully in a space that smells only of him. A second ticks by, a minute, an eternity, and then his lips brush against mine. I respond, mimicking their movements.

A content sigh escapes him, and his tense body relaxes against mine. The kiss deepens as he tilts his head to the side, giving his tongue better access to mine. They tangle and twirl, a dance of their own. The taste of him explodes across my tongue.

The hand at my back tightens and he pulls me flush against him. Needing skin contact, I slip my fingers under his shirt and trail them along his skin. His skin is soft and silky, an inviting combination. I push my hand up further and feel my way around the muscles across his back.

I break the kiss momentarily, our breaths releasing in heavy huffs that further heat the space around us. His lips are swollen, rounded in a way that tells me he's about to speak.

Before he can utter a word, I grab the hem of his shirt and lift it over his head. The glow in his eyes is filled with such passionate desire, such determination and possession, that the mental wall I've built to keep him out crumbles. He blinks in a slow motion, his long lashes fanning his under-eye. Then, his hands return to me, lifting my own shirt over my head and unsnapping my bra with a single flick of his wrist. My bra falls to the floor next to my shirt, a soft rustle of fabric.

He takes his time letting his gaze wander over my bare skin, soaking me in, memorizing every detail. My nipples harden further at the touchless attention.

He snaps from his perusal and lowers his mouth down on mine. The kiss is frenzied, his hands gripping both sides of my face as he devours my lips. I respond in kind.

I fumble with the button of his pants before it finally unhooks. Unzipping it, I push the slacks down as far as I can reach without breaking the kiss. He kicks off his shoes, steps out of the pants, and uses his foot to fling them away.

Pushing me back against the car, his body applying pressure and angling over mine, his hands leave my face as he rids me of my pants. They pool on the floor around my shoes.

He slows the kissing, becoming more sensual and directing it with careful strokes of his tongue. His hands travel up my sides to the swell of my breasts and back down to my hips. The trail of heat they leave behind is undeniable.

Hooking a finger on each side of my panties, he slips them off. They fall like silk.

He breaks the kiss. "I'm going to enjoy this, Ira. I hope you're a patient girl because I plan to take my time."

My clit twitches at his admission.

He gently pecks my neck, making imprints of wet, hot, sensual brushes from my collar bone to the top of my breasts. When his tongue slides around my left nipple in a slow manner, I moan.

Goosebumps cover my breasts, sweeping heat to my lower abdomen. He pauses, chuckles a little, then flicks his tongue. I grab his hair and push him closer my nipple, wordlessly begging him to relieve the ache settling there.

He clicks his tongue. "I'll be directing this orchestra, Ira."

He flicks his tongue again, then scrapes his teeth across my nipple. Using his other hand, he tweaks the other, the pain such a pleasure. My head falls back momentarily, another moan escaping my mouth. My clit throbs and pulses.

After a minute of pure torture, he captures my nipple and sucks, rapidly flicking his tongue against it. I grip his shoulders, my nails digging in. The heat of his mouth, the pull of his suck, the electric currents from the assault, make my inner walls pulsate.

He moves his mouth to the other nipple, repeating the same torment. When I begin to squirm, he finally trails kisses down my stomach. He lowers himself further and further, squatting in front of me.

Reaching my mound, he traces his tongue down the sides where it meets my thighs. I exhale my discomfort, my need almost painful.

He glances up at me. A smug smile tugs at his lips. Without looking he unbuckles my shoes and slips them off, followed by my pants and underwear that are still pooled around my ankles.

I spread my legs, wordlessly telling him what I want. What I need.

His knees rest on the ground and he uses his fingers to spread my lips. I watch the erotic scene unfold, heavy breaths making my breasts rise and fall. He holds my eyes before he dives forward, sucking my clit and gently flicking his tongue as he does so.

I moan and bury my hands in his hair. The scene is too much—sensationally unreal—to look away. I watch as his wet tongue slides across the swollen bud. A jolt of hot electricity zaps to every sensitive part of my flesh, and I buck against his mouth.

Using one hand to keep my lips spread, he pushes a finger into me. I cry out, my legs quivering from the intrusion. My walls clamp around it, holding it in place as he rubs inside me.

The heat boils in my lower abdomen, coiling and begging for release. Soft, breathy moans escape my mouth. "Flint . . ." I whimper, begging him to release the heat.

He shoves another finger inside and roughly pumps his hand up and down. Tugging his hair, I wordlessly demand, beg, and whimper.

More heat coils, stirs, builds, and then explodes. A pitchy groan, loud to my ears, develops deep within my chest and travels right out of my mouth. My fingers loosen their grip on his hair, running through the strands instead—a gentle caress. Warm liquid spreads over his fingers as I pulsate around them.

His pumps slow as my climax fades. He retracts his fingers and stands up, leaving my wet clit to the exposed air.

The walls of my sex continuously grip nothing, missing the fingers that stretched them. My body isn't done. My body isn't ready for the pleasure to be over, and by the smile on his face, I think that he knows that. Scents it, even.

Flint presses his body back against mine. My nipples brush against his bare chest, his erection pressing against my abdomen, and he kisses me, forcing me to taste myself. He keeps the kiss slow, sensual, while I frantically try to push down his underwear. They hit the floor and he kicks them away.

Lifting my leg around his waist, he rocks his erection against my swollen parts, and I groan into his mouth. Slow, tortured pressure continues as his shaft rubs, and rubs, and rubs. His precum drips below my belly button and he moans into my mouth.

Heat coils again, the wicked assault so soon after my first climax, my clit already so sensitive. It builds with each rock of his hips, each rub, and I explode a second time. His mouth muffles my cries as he continues to rock.

My climax subsides, my legs quivering from all the effort.

Gripping my ass, he hoists the other leg over his hip and lifts me, never breaking the kiss. I tower over him while he carries me to his chosen destination. Using the added height to my advantage, I kiss him deeper, my tongue fighting for battle. I keep a firm grip on his hair and he places me on a hard surface—the garage's workbench.

Once seated, I wrap my fingers around his length and pump my hand. He moans into my mouth, and a shiver spreads through his body. It excites me, and I pump faster, his own fingers circling my wrist and gripping tightly. Then, he directs my hand and positions his dick at my entrance. Slowly, with carefully measured practice, he inserts the tip and pushes inside. His hip bones meet my inner thighs when he's fully sheathed, my walls clamping around him and refusing to let go.

He sighs a groan. "So wet, so warm," he murmurs against my lips.

He looks into my eyes while he pulls out and slides back in. I grip the counter by both sides of my hips and lean back slightly so I can watch his dick disappear. He pulls back again, moaning and cursing, and slowly slides back in. The counter rocks as he does so, aiding him in the motion. My breasts jiggle each time he rocks, only adding to the erotic sight.

In . . . out . . . in . . . out. Each movement rubs against my swollen insides, the heat building once more. My breaths quicken, but by now, he knows what that means. "Cum for me, Ira."

I glance back into his eyes. His jaw is set, his face is firm, and he watches the reaction I'm having to his actions. My chest rises and falls in exaggerated motions and the heat releases. My walls become slick once more as it slides over his dick, and my scream echoes throughout the spacious garage.

"Fuck," Flint growls, pumping his hips faster, sending me into an orgasm. My cries of pleasure continue as I ride the waves of it. My walls pull and pull, and his fingers dig into my hips. He slams home one last time when he finds his own release. Several mumbled, "Oh God," and "shit," leaves his lips.

My orgasm subsides, but my heavy breathing remains. The pulsating stills and his eyes lift back to mine. Warmth spreads through me, a warmth that has nothing to do with pleasure. I blink to it, knowing exactly what it means. The beginning of the mating is clicking into place.

This new and unexplored warmth fills an ache within me. It replaces a discomfort I didn't know was there. I feel whole, sane, without trouble. And suddenly . . . the world makes sense. My purpose feels set, and I know – *I know* – this is where I belong.

A small smile spreads across his lips, smug about finally having me.

But reality hits and the consequences of what I've done slams home. I hold my breath.

What have I done?

CHAPTER NINE

Flint Rockland

Dyson, Romaine, and I stand around the fire ring. Thousands of sparkling, twinkling stars dot and pattern the black sky, the full moon the only thing lighting our world. It calls to my wolf—he's eager to play and bask in the moon's beams. I ignore his urges for now, not fully trusting him yet. At least he's been quiet the last few hours.

Since Irene and I began the mating, his mood has made a drastic change. He feels as protective as ever, but not for my life. No, his protectiveness has shifted from me to our mate. A part of me feels grateful. The other part of me is worried. Will he obsess over her safety as much as he did for me? I worry if his paranoia will return, and if it does, what it will do to Irene.

Readying the pit for the bonfire, Romaine situates the wood just so, grunting as he leans to grab more logs from a pile to his left. I shift my gaze to Irene who sits with the rest of the pack on the back porch. She holds my gaze while answering something Kenna has asked her. Her arms are crossed over her chest, her eyebrows slightly pinched. She's upset. Why, I'm not sure. I'm pulled away before I can investigate further.

Romaine slaps me on the back. "Congratulations, man."

I nod my thanks to him, a small smile lifting my cheeks.

Dyson shifts uncomfortably beside me. I spare him a glance before returning my attention to Romaine. "How are you settling in?"

He nods his head. "Good. It's a far stretch from where we came from. I'm grateful for you guys taking us in, by the way. Not a lot of packs would do that."

This time, I slap him on the back. "It's good to have you."

Victoria, one of the new wolves, calls his name from the open kitchen window. Romaine hands me the matches before gripping my shoulder in a meaningful gesture. His eyes pointedly flick to Dyson, and then he takes off at a jog.

A deep breath forces its way through my nose, and I turn to Dyson. *Round three.* "How are you holding up?"

Dyson shifts his weight again. "I'm doing alright," he says, his voice emotionless. He's lying. An idiot would be able to tell that he's only telling me what I want to hear.

I go to light the fire, thinking over my next words carefully so he doesn't walk away. I can't continue

144

to hold this grudge. I've got a mate to think about now. Holding onto the past . . . I don't want to do it anymore.

Lighting wadded newspaper under the logs, I stand back and watch as it is engulfed in flames. "Look, man, I'm sorry."

Dyson stiffens and glances at me. "For what?"

"For taking all this," I wave my hand around in a small circle, "out on you. That wasn't fair of me. You went through the same shit I did."

Dyson holds his stare, his expression blank. I briefly glance at him before returning my eyes to the growing fire. The flames lick up the logs, and the bark along the logs start to glow.

"Thanks," he finally says in a quiet voice.

I bump my shoulder against his, feeling more like myself than I have in months. "So, what have you been up to?"

Dyson shrugs and turns to the fire. "Not a whole lot. Research. A lot of video games, I guess. Trying to get right with myself."

I nod. I understand that.

"What about you?" he asks.

I shrug. "Also trying to screw my head on straight."

The silence stretches on and the sound of an owl hooting in the woods fills it. "How's your wolf?" Dyson mumbles. "I'm sorry I didn't visit you when he was like that. I should have, but I figured it'd make it worse."

It probably would have. Even now, my wolf is keeping a close eye on Dyson, not fully trusting him.

"He's fine. The mating has calmed him down." I switch the subject and paste a smile on my face. "You ready for a fire?"

Dyson shifts his weight around in an antsy sort of way. "Actually, I have an errand to run, but I'll be back."

Before I can ask him about this errand and his nervousness, he squeezes my shoulder. "I love you, man. Treat your mate right, okay? Don't waste a moment with her." He leaves, striding off to the parking garage. I watch, frowning, as he walks, his head lowered and his hands in his pockets.

I have no plans of going back to my old lifestyle. That person no longer exists. My mate will get more than she deserves. I'll see to that. But why did his advice feel like a nail in a coffin?

Irene Scott

Evo kisses Kenna on the cheek and lifts himself off his chair. He heads down the deck toward Flint. Dyson had just left, and Flint is still staring at the space where he once was. There's hurt in his eyes, and I almost wish I was close enough to hear whatever they were saying to each other.

Slapping Flint on the back, Evo joins him by the fire. He stuffs his hands in his pockets and strikes up a conversation. The rest of the men follow, shoving each other jokingly down the steps and laughing all the way over to the flames.

The women remain quiet around me, content on watching the men be men.

The fire blazes, its orange fingers licking the air. A fire is always hungry, never satisfied, and I watch it for a moment, completely transfixed.

Flint angles himself to fully face Evo, and I get the full profile of his face. He smiles, his white teeth glinting in the pale moon light. The shadowing flickers of the fire dance across him. And when Flint laughs, the throaty noise full of joy reaches my ears and fills my heart. How can my heart possibly hold so much?

I love him.

I frown, dread damping my abrupt revelation. But I shouldn't love him. I can't love him. I made a deal with Jazz. I must choose between my brother . . . or my mate. Do I betray this pack and the one I love? Or do I save my own flesh and blood, heeding to the demands of my enemy?

My wolf howls inside me, disgusted with the deal I've made with the devil. Disgusted that there's even an option in the first place. Disgusted that my life feels a little bit like a hungry fire.

My eyebrows soften.

But I do. I do love him. And that love could consume everything I've worked so hard to hide and accomplish.

Flint Rockland

Ira and I sit on top of a light blue blanket that covers the ground. The pack surrounds the fire, telling stories and laughing at memories. Ira, snug between my legs, listens with interest, nestling deeper into my chest.

She's been oddly quiet while listening to her friend, Kat, the witch who owns the shop in town. The witch has been chatting about a thieving customer, and her animated hand gestures are keeping everyone's interest.

Romaine, who sits next to Kat, watches her with intense curiosity and admiration. I'm not sure if he's ever seen a witch, but it's obvious he's interested in more ways than one.

His eyes travel the length of her tattooed body, then back to her pixie-like face, studying every feature. He feels my gaze and lifts his eyes to meet mine. A slow smile spreads across my face before he matches it. He shrugs and shifts his body back toward the pit.

Kat seems like she talks excessively just to fill the space. A nervous habit? Possibly. She had been discussing how she rid the thief from her shop using a well-placed electro-current spell.

I cut her off mid-sentence. "So how does your magic work, exactly?"

Irene straightens up a little, interested in the information Kat may provide.

Kat shrugs. "We're descendants of Erline . . . or Mother Nature, as you call her. We're tied to her by blood and inherited a fraction of her daughter's gifts."

Mother Nature has a daughter? Or had? I cock my head to the side.

Kenna huffs. "Mother Nature," she mumbles under her breath, her eyes narrowing.

"Oh, she's real." Kat nods, her nose piercing glittering in the fire's light. "I've met her."

Irene's head raises a tad, her voice skeptical. "You've met her? Mother Nature?"

"Erline," she corrects before scratching the back of her neck. "Not on the best of terms, she and I."

I raise an eyebrow and stroke Irene's thigh absentmindedly. "Oh? Did you cut down one of her trees and craft a wand?"

Ben and Romaine chuckle.

Kat shrugs, averting her gaze. Her deflection piques my curiosity further, but I can tell I offended her.

"Tell me about your legends," Irene says, coming to her friend's defense by getting back to the topic at hand. She snuggles back in, awaiting the new twist to the stories being told tonight.

Kat looks around the fire and meets everyone's gaze. Fire dances in her eyes as the pack settles in and patiently waits for the tales of a witch's life.

She exhales and rolls her neck. "It all begins in the medieval ages of France when the first born witch was born," she looks at Irene pointedly, "that's our ancestry—French folks adapted many myths and legends: Greek, Norse, even Germanic. But the legends and myths were just that. They were conjured for the purpose of explaining away how and why things happened and came to be." She shrugs. "They're humans, ya know? They didn't really know any different."

She pauses, the fire crackling. "Erline is the Fee in charge of this Realm. She created it, just like all the Fee of every realm."

"Fee?" Victoria asks, sitting up a little straighter and cocking an eyebrow.

Kat squints as she looks over the top of the fire. "Fae, or faeries, as fiction literature calls it. Fee is French for Fae. We've never changed it. To us witches, they've always been and will always be Fee." Victoria nods and leans back into her lawn chair. Kat continues, "The Fee control everything. They govern over the realms they've created like unseen kings and queens." Her nose twitches and she rubs it. "Sometimes they make themselves known to the humans on the Earth Realm, which is why the humans believed them to be Gods so long ago. Not too far of a stretch if you ask me. They can be quite intimidating and self-righteous."

"How do you know all this?" Evo interrupts, resting his arms on the armrest and holding his chin with his hand.

Kenna slaps his chest with the back of her hand. "Let her finish."

Kenna nods at Kat to keep going. "Like I said, there are many realms. One Fee," she holds up a finger, "is in charge of each realm. Our stories say that, long ago, Erline craved more. Though all before her is of her design, she wanted a child of her own. She saw all that she created and watched them procreate new life. With the help of Kheelan, the Fee of the Death Realm, they gave birth to a child," she pauses the story, taking a deep breath while staring at the fire, remembering all the details that had once been told to her. The fire crackles, sending sparks into the sky.

"Her name was Myla." Kat's voice is lower, softer. "She was the first born witch. The story is long and chaotic, but eventually and inevitably, Erline hid Myla from Kheelan. She didn't want her only daughter in the hands of a Fee who craved death for fear that Myla's magic would be used for destructive purposes."

Kenna clears her throat. "What, exactly, can the Fee do?"

Kat laughs and sweeps out her arm. "All that you see before you. Great magic. Terrible magic. A witch's magic holds nothing compared to theirs. Nothing compared to the first born witch's, either."

I raise an eyebrow, skeptical. "How come we've never heard of this. I mean, I get why the humans are kept in the dark, but why are the shifters?"

151

She shrugs, her small shoulders bobbing. "Information gets lost if it isn't passed down through the generations. Witches are more sentimental. History is practically bred into us."

"So, if you're a descendant, what does that make us—the shifters?" Bre asks.

"Her creation," she answers in a quiet voice.

It's silent for a moment before someone asks another question. Bre asks, "And the vampires?"

Kat fiddles with the hem of her jeans. "The vampires are not living beings. They're not created by Erline. She only holds power over the living."

"What about ghosts?" I ask, a cocky smirk on my face.

"Same rules apply. This isn't their realm, but some are stuck here. I don't know everything, Flint." She tilts her head to me, narrowing her eyes. "And they prefer to be called shades, by the way."

"So . . . they would be Kheelan's creation?" I ask, trying like hell to connect the dots of her tangled legends.

Kat sighs, annoyed with my disbelief. "Sort of. Kheelan doesn't create the shades, only the vampires. He just . . . governs over them."

"Why did he create the vampires?" Irene asks.

"Well, when he couldn't find his daughter, he was furious. He created the vampires and sent them to this realm to search for her. Obviously," she waves her hand in the air, "they never found her, but they remained in this realm anyway."

I snort. Of course, they did. There's a free supply of blood here.

"How many realms are there?" Evalyn asks in a whisper. Those are the first words I've ever heard her speak. Her voice is crackly with age.

Kat returns her attention to the fire. "There's a few," she whispers. "Some have angels. Some have sandmen. And some even have demons."

I watch the fire, picturing the tale Kat painted while inserting creatures of pure legend roaming lands I'll never visit. The flames flare when a breeze pushes across the dark lawn. I glance at Kat who watches as well, and I swear, just for a moment, that the flames bend toward her. Maybe I'm imagining things—the blaze and the legend playing tricks on my mind.

How is this a real story? A real legend? A real piece of history? I don't like that there's an indication of more powerful beings. My wolf doesn't either, even if Erline is the creator of my kind. People with immense power can be dangerous and should be watched over so their power isn't abused. How do you watch someone who you never knew existed?

Irene lightly nudges me in the stomach with her elbow. "Where's Dyson?"

I glance around, realizing he isn't here. "I thought he'd be back by now."

Bre perks up from within her chair, her gaze to mine from across the fire. "Where'd he go, anyway?"

My shoulders lift as I shrug, jostling Irene. "An errand, I guess."

Bre frowns and looks at Ben. He shrugs his own shoulders, the lawn chair creaking as he does so. We remain quiet, concern on all our faces. Packs are close-knit. None of us enjoy the idea of not knowing where a pack mate is. I should have asked more questions before he left.

Kenna shivers and Bre stands up and stretches. She holds out her hand to Kenna. "Come on. Time for you to head inside."

Kenna frowns at her outstretched hand. "I'm not a fragile China doll. I can lift myself out of the chair."

Jessup and Evalyn, the mated couple, snuggle deeper into each other and watch with the rest of us as Kenna shimmies her way to the end of the seat. Evo places his chin back in his hand and hides a smile behind his fingers. Kenna curses as the chair almost tips over, and Irene chuckles with Victoria.

I sigh contently when Irene rubs her cheek against my chest and breathes in my scent. Then, she eases herself off the ground. "I'm going to go in with them and check on the baby before she goes to sleep."

I nod as she heads off with Bre, Kenna, and Kat. I assume Kat will leave shortly. She and Irene seem to be good friends, and I make a mental note to ask Irene how that friendship came about.

With the four women gone, the rest of us listen to the roar of the fire and the crickets chirping their song. A slight breeze ruffles my short hair and I scratch my head at the unwelcome tickle.

Abruptly, Evo snaps his head up. His eyes narrow and his body tenses.

Alerted, Ben asks, "What is it?"

He remains quiet, scanning the trees, before speaking in a hushed tone, "The crickets."

I look at the trees. The bugs have ceased their song. The hair on the back of my neck stands on end, and I slowly rise to my feet. Everyone else follows suit.

"Nobody move," Evo whispers.

My breaths, my rapid heart rate, the breeze—it's the only thing I can hear, but . . .

A twig snaps. I whip my gaze to the left where the trees cast the deepest shadows. The breeze shifts, carrying a distinct scent to my nose.

"Shit," I growl.

CHAPTER TEN

Irene Scott

After checking Kenna, I softly shut the door to the Alpha's room and blow out a breath. Through the door, I can hear Brenna talking softly to Kenna. She had wanted to stay behind and tend to Kenna's needs, ensuring that she stays in bed and actually gets a good night's rest.

Kat, leaning against the white wall in the hallway, pushes off and descends the stairs with me.

"You have a bathroom around here?" she asks, peeking around the corner of the kitchen.

I nod with my back still to her. I continue putting one foot in front of the other, my destination being the fridge while a numb sort of feeling overcomes me, knowing that what Jazz asked of me will soon have to be fulfilled. "In the living room."

Her footsteps retreat back the way we came, and soon after, the bathroom door clicks shut. I open the fridge, grab a plastic bottle of water, and leave the door open as I twist off the lid. A big sigh escapes my lips.

Kenna is dilated. I'm going to have to call Reese. It shouldn't be long before that baby makes its arrival and screams its outrage to the cold world.

What the hell am I going to do? How am I to snatch a baby with an entire pack around? Even if I manage to, I'll be condemning an innocent, hours old, child to the fate of rogues. I'm not capable of such malevolent acts. This is too much. *It's too much.*

I lift the bottle to my lips, but it flies from my hands as my body sails through the air and smashes into the nearby wall. The condiments in the fridge door crash to the floor. The splatter from the contents of my water bottle splashes on every surface. The bottle lands in a pile of pickle jar glass, and its lid rolls to the cabinets below the sink.

Before I have a moment to adjust—to discover what had hurled me like discarded garbage— fingers wrap around my throat, slamming my head against the wall. The drywall cracks and the wall moans on impact. Instinctively, I claw at the fingers with desperation, and then look my attacker in the eye.

Red eyes glow back at me. *A vampire.*

The smell of death and rotting flesh fans my face, and two very sharp and pointed fangs drip spittle as the vampire hisses. Black veins zigzag under his pale skin and fear roils in my stomach.

I remove my hands from prying away the vampire's grip and flatten my fingers. In a quick motion—one that matches his own speed—I slap my palms over his ears. Vampires have sensitive hearing, just like shifters do. The audible slap rings true, echoing through the room, and his hands loosen from their grasp. I grab the boney fingers, twist his arm, and flip him to the ground.

There's a howl coming from outside, a clear warning. My heart thuds a little faster. This isn't a singled-out attack, a slip past defenses. We—this entire pack—are under attack.

A bone in his arm crunches as he hits the floor with a thud. I'm emotionally thrown by his lack of pain when he chuckles from his sprawled-out position. I suppose when you're dead, so are your nerves. Either that or he's just another insane creature roaming this world.

Distracted by his laugh, my grip loosens, and he yanks his broken arm free. He uses his other arm, wraps his cold, boney fingers around my leg, and pulls. I crash to the ground with him. I smack my head against the wood planks and speckled stars creep into my vision. I double blink, trying to dispel them, and silently degrade myself.

In a blur of speed, the vampire is on top of me. His brown, straw-like hair is tousled from his time spent on the floor, and his arm dangles at an odd angle at his side.

He hisses in my face, more spittle splatting against my cheek. He leans down and I get a better view of his eyes, pools of red liquid . . . like several shades of the blood he drinks.

"I have a message," he says, the words distorted as his lips slide over his fangs. His voice is void of emotion. I try to wiggle loose, but his thighs keep my arms locked in place. "Bring the baby or the pack dies. She doesn't care if you have to cut him out. Do your job."

I grit my teeth and lean away from his decaying scent. "I don't know what you're talking about."

His veiny eyelids narrow over the pools of red liquid. "If you truly think you have a choice . . . Choose wisely, little wolf."

The ground rumbles and vibrates beneath my back. The vampire searches the floor for the cause. He stands, unsure of the movement. Once he's to his feet, I peer between his legs.

There, in the entrance to the kitchen, Kat stands. Her right arm is raised, palm up, and her lips move in quick motions as she whispers something into the atmosphere. The groaning of the floor overpowers her whispered words, but magic thickens in the air.

Her eyes, her face . . . it transforms. Her cheekbones stick out farther than normal—boney and the skin darkening to the color of bruises. Her eyelids are as black as night, and each of her once perfect teeth spike from their gums in pointed arrows.

I've heard about what a witch looks like when she's using magic. I heard the tales, but I never . . .

Splintering wood flies into the air as thick, deep green vines spring free. The floorboards continue to quake and moan.

Kat bends her elbow, then shoves her hand forward, palm facing the vampire. Impossible winds whip around her short pixie hair before they reach me, howling past the island as they come. I grip the post on the island to keep myself from flying around with the winds.

Cabinet doors open and shut, stools soar across the floor, and the contents of the counters tumble past my head. I duck, avoiding the contact.

The vampire, desperately trying to keep his own feet on the ground, whips his head around, facing the vines poised to strike. The vines lash forward and snake around his torso. They continue wrapping around him like a cocoon, lifting him into the air.

The vampire hisses and shrieks while trying to wriggle free. The winds now more centered around the vines and their victim, and I stand, stumbling away from the event unfolding. Carefully, using the edge of the island, I move across the shaking floor until I can see his face.

The vines wrap around his neck, dive through his open mouth, and shoot straight down his throat. Leaves, splinters, and feet of vine forcefully bury themselves inside of him. His screeching transforms into guttural sounds, the vampire's eyes wide as he watches Kat. I can only guess at the vine's destination, but my theory is it's wrapping itself around his dead heart. The vampire stiffens suddenly and stops wiggling; his expression is one of pain and shock, and then . . .

He bursts into ash and dust.

Several breathes leave my flared nostrils in heavy huffs. In my peripheral vision, Kat's hand lowers back to her side, shoulders rising and falling with her own fast breathing. The vines drop to the floor in a heap and the winds disappear entirely.

Swallowing thickly, I blink at the black ash piled underneath the vines, my mind works frantically to piece together what I've just witnessed. I've never seen a witch use her abilities, I've never seen the monstrous face they have when they do, either. Not while fighting. Not while defending themselves, and even so, I've never heard of a witch doing *that.*

I turn to Kat. Her eyes glow around the rim of her brown irises—a shade of orange. I frown. Witch's eyes glow? I thought that was just a shifter trait.

Kat meets my gaze, her expression blank, her frightening features holding their place.

"What are you?" I ask, a notch above a whisper.

She blinks and the orange rim disappears. "I heard what he said. What choice do you have to make, Ira?" she asks, deflecting my question with one of her own. "What did he mean?"

Taken aback by the sudden switch of subject, I back up a step, as if struck. My mind is still trying to work out what I just witnessed. The vines, the earth moving, the wind—that's all part of nature, right? Her face . . . I just didn't realize how strong witches are. Or maybe it's just *this* witch. And the glowing eyes—I know for a fact her eyes didn't glow when she performed Kenna and Bre's unity service.

I rub at my eyebrows, trying to piece things together.

"The vampire. He said you had a choice. What did he mean?"

"I have no idea," I lie and avert my gaze from her intimidating features.

We scream at the sound of glass shattering and crashing to the ground. The shards skitter across the dining room floor before the shards come to a twirling halt.

I move quickly to Kat's side. Within the shards of what was once the sliding glass door, another vampire scrambles to his feet. Deep red blood, almost black in color, seeps from several small cuts, but like the other, he doesn't seem to feel it. Or seem to care.

Evo barges in. His shoes crunch against the glass, and his eyes glow wolf in his partially shifted state. With clawed hands, he grabs the vampire's shoulders and slams him onto the dining table. The wood groans and splinters from the force. The vampire clambers, trying to escape out from under Evo's iron grasp.

Evo roars, plunging his clawed hand into the chest of the vampire. The vampire stills as Evo's fingers wrap around his heart. He dusts like the other when the organ is crushed, and Evo's hand remains where it was before the vampire's death, knuckles resting on the broken table.

His shoulders rise and fall, and then he turns glowing eyes to us while shaking the dust from his hand. A frown dips his blond eyebrows when he peers at the destruction behind us.

"You okay?" he asks. His shirt is in tatters, but his skin remains unscathed.

I nod, and then jump when a screech comes from the other room.

"What the fuck is going on?" Kenna yells. She walks into view dressed in a nightgown, and her long brown hair into a messy bun. Bre holds onto her elbow as she waddles her way to us. She takes in the full view, starting with the open area where the sliding door once was. "What the fuck!"

"Kenna, go back to our room," Evo warns, his head twisting behind him to the battle happening out on the lawn. He searches the scene, and for a moment, we listen to the chaos. My heart skips a beat, unsure of the well-being of my mate.

"I will not," she growls, her eyes glowing. She grits her teeth. "Tell me what is happening, Evo."

"A hoard of vampires," he starts, before backing up to exit the way he came. He points a clawed finger at her. "Stay here, Kenna. Brenna, don't let her leave." He turns and heads back outside.

All is silent inside the house. The only noise is our heavy breathing and sounds of the snarls and hissing outside.

Something slams into the siding of the house. It breaks me from my trance, and my mind comes to a quick conclusion. I slowly, numbly, make my way through the broken glass, the shards crunching under my shoes. Kat follows close behind me.

"What are you doing?" Brenna hisses.

I momentarily stop in my tracks, my tone wavering. "I'm not staying in here. Not when I – I can help them!"

A howl sounds through the night and I make my way a little faster, taking extra care not to slip.

"Fuck this shit," Kenna growls. She and Bre follow us out, Bre's arm linked with hers to make sure she doesn't fall. I'm sure they are just as worried about their mates as I am about mine, but I hadn't expected company – unity. I had anticipated them to listen to their alpha.

I step onto the deck. The noise is much louder out here, graver and more terrible. I breathe deep and long. Everything, even sounds, are occurring in slow motion as my thoughts try to catch up with my adrenaline. The vampire's threat repeats over and over again, a broken record to remind me of everything I have to lose.

"Holy shit," Kat and Kenna say together.

A few Cloven Pack shifters have shifted to protect their territory. Others remain partially shifted. In the blur of speed and the dark of night, it's difficult to tell who is who.

The fire still crackles from within the pit, a forgotten blaze roaring to life as vampire limbs are tossed into it as soon as they're ripped from the bodies. Vampires can live without their limbs, this I know.

The blankets and chairs are still in the same position as they were left. It's a strange sight to see those chairs unharmed. To know that moments ago, our world was calm and full of magical, mythical tales. And now . . .

Two wolves attack a vampire, ripping him to pieces. A wolf pauses to howl, victory in his kill. I squint to see who it is. It could be any of the males, but the shadows fold around the howling beast like liquid. Evo holds another in a chokehold while Ben buries his hand into his chest. The vampire ashes quickly. My eyes move, scanning the wolves, looking for Flint, desperately flitting from wolf to wolf, person to person.

I find him and zero in. He remains in his human form—a bold move or one out of fear—as a hoard of vampires pick up on his unprotected status. They stalk, swarming around him in a circle.

My fingers curl into my palms. Why isn't he shifting?

Hurriedly, I rush to the stairs and I grip the rail. My footsteps thunder down each step as I make my way to the lawn. The smell of vampire blood hits me at the same time my shoe touches the grass.

Kat follows, chanting words behind me. The ground rumbles and rolls in waves. It skirts around me and stretches beyond, sending the vampires attempting to corner my mate to the ground.

Noticing that Flint is surrounded, three wolves come out of nowhere. Each pounce, burying their muzzles into the vampires' ribcage. The sounds of their bones breaking reach my ears. It makes my hair stand on end and goosebumps rise on my skin.

Now close to the mass, and by smell, I identify the three wolves as Victoria, Romaine, and Darla.

I snarl and partially shift as the remaining vampires move closer to Flint before Victoria, Romaine, or Darla can get to them. Without adjusting their tattered and rumpled clothes, their muscles tense, ready to spring at my unprotected mate.

In my peripheral vision, I see something glow. My eyes shift toward it, distracted by its light. A ball of flames rest on Kat's palm. It licks her skin, twirls and swirls. She stares in amazement while the flames stroke her, leaving her without burns.

Shocked, Kat glances up at me. The neon orange rims are back and surrounding her irises. I double blink, making sure I'm seeing what I'm actually seeing. Witches shouldn't be able to conjure nature—they can only use what's already there, be it buried in the dirt, or risen above the grass. What is she hiding?

Before I can comment, the remaining vampires move, but not at Flint. No. They've turned their attention to me – the girl whose attention is elsewhere. They charge at me, but Flint beats them to it. He partially shifts on the spot, and when he reaches me, he shoves me behind him. His muscles flex in his back as he roars at the fanged creatures.

Kat, snapping out of her shock, throws her flaming ball. It hits the first vampire and engulfs him in an unnatural flame. The vampire screams as he burns in slow agony, the flames taking their time with its victim.

My eyes zoom in on the risen vampires stalking in our direction. My wolf pounds against his cage, demanding to be free to protect his salvation—his mate. *Our mate.*

I push Irene further behind me. If only she stayed inside!

I pay no mind to one of the vampires engulfed in flames. My focus is only on the others who stare hungrily at my mate.

Two charge me. Ben, now in wolf form—a blur of black fur—tackles one of them to the ground. The other continues on, a blur of speed. I bend and lean my weight into it. His torso hits my side and he tumbles over my back. The force of the vampire's impact drops him to the ground. A roar rips from my throat, my sanity slipping. He jumps up, ready for another round, while the rest of my pack takes care of the others who had stalked me, and then my mate.

The vampire lashes out with his pointed black nails. I lean backward, narrowly missing it. He swings again. I block the swing with an open fist, and with my other hand, I bury my claws deep inside his chest. His insides are like ribbons of ice, his cold heart thick as the head of a rubber mallet in my grip.

The vampire stills, but I keep him suspended between his present, undead state and his final death. His eyes widen, realizing his presence on this world has come to an end.

My lips slightly curve around my sharp canines and I yank the organ from his chest. It comes out with a sound similar to the ripping of a newspaper.

His mouth opens and closes while he clutches at the empty hole, staring at the heart I now hold in my hands. His face cracks in fright.

I glance down at the heart, examining it, my smirk turning into a grin while shifting the organ this way and that. Goo drips from the black heart and my fingertips as I take in all the curves and veins.

Victory courses through my body, vibrating my bones and sending a rush of adrenaline through my veins. I gradually squeeze the dead organ. The unnecessary breath seizes in the vampire and his deep, red eyes go wild and helpless, almost . . . pleading.

Roaring with outrage, I crush the heart in my hand. It instantly turns to dust and I watch as he flakes away. Almost as if he never existed, the wind takes his pieces and they drift away with the breeze, disappearing from my sight and into the black night.

The world around me is quiet . . . too quiet. I breathe in short, shallow gasps. My chest expands to its limit, the air rushing from both my mouth and nostrils. My arms quiver as I try to control my wolf. He howls and snarls and bangs against his cage. I squeeze my eyes shut and give my head a little shake. The mental effort to keep him contained is proving difficult and the more I try, the more it hurts.

Irene moves to stand before me. Her scent is enough for me to open my eyes, and when I do, I find her searching my face warily. She takes a careful step closer and reaches a hand to touch my face, but I lean away from her fingers.

"Don't," I grumble around my wolf's teeth.

She stops her advance, her hand suspended in mid-air before she lowers it back to her side. "Flint . . ." she begins, her voice soft and wary.

A shiver ripples down my spine. I groan as my wolf persists, my clawed fingers balling into fists.

"Should Irene be near him when he's like that?" Kat asks. Someone mumbles an incoherent reply.

Irene's eyes wander over my shaking frame, her hands searching the air – the space between us – for a way to ease me. "Just breathe," she eventually whispers. "Deep breaths."

Abruptly, she places her fumbling hands over her heart, then mimics the breaths she wants me to make. Her shoulders rise and fall over and over again. "Come on, Flint. Try."

I suck in a deep, shaky breath, and release it just the same.

Breathe, I chant to myself.

My heart rate slows as I continue to watch her shoulders rise and fall. My chest mimics her rhythm, soothing my wolf.

Irene takes a tentative and tiny step closer to me. When I don't stop her advance, she readjusts her hand over my thudding heart, her fingers caressing the surface. The heat and pressure of her palm eases me further. Her scent swirls around my head, reaching my wolf and reminding me of who I am.

His growling and snarling quiets as he takes notice of his mate, unharmed and alert.

In his pause, the world returns. The crickets chirp, the stars twinkle, and my pack mates inch closer. It doesn't take long before I can shift fully back to my human form.

My lungs beg for more oxygen, but I continue with Irene's instructions. Slowly, my breaths return to normal and my wolf retreats deep within me.

When my eyes stop glowing, she sags with relief and wraps her arms around my waist. Her head replaces her hand over my heart, and she listens to it thud against my ribs.

Taking the moment, I place my nose in her hair and drink her in. Her scent tickles my senses, and I find . . . I find that my heart beats only for her.

You never know how deep love runs until someone yanks you from your darkest hour. To take your hand from inside the grave you've dug for yourself and bring you to the surface to suck in that fresh air once more. To save you from yourself. To not run for the hills but save a soul instead. It's a debt you can never repay. It's the ultimate, selfless sacrifice. She's my only salvation.

It's at this moment that I know I'll never be able to repay her. That she doesn't deserve me. But I'll selfishly never let her go. I'll spend the rest of my life loving this woman and hope that that's enough. It's all I've got to give—my unwavering metaphorical heart.

Because I love her.

With Irene in my arms, I look to my pack. Evo and Ben nod at me, the set of their eyebrows relaxing. But there, struggling between their grasps, is a vampire. His pale skin shines brightly under the moon's beam.

Romaine catches me glaring at the vampire and comments, "Hostage," while tilting his head in that direction.

"How did this happen?" I ask no one in particular.

Bre and Kenna reach the pack, Kenna huffing as she waddles. Beads of sweat sprinkle her forehead. "I'd like to know the same damn thing," she growls.

Irene flinches in my arms. I glance down at her, her hands sticking to my sweaty shirt as she nuzzles in deeper.

"Calm down," Evo mumbles. "It's not good for the baby." He passes the vampire's arm off to Romaine, and he and Ben take the hostage toward the garage. The vampire hisses and lunges, but a well-aimed punch from Ben knocks him out.

"I'll calm down as soon as someone tells me what a bunch of walking, blood-sucking, dead guys are doing on our lawn." Her gaze switches to Irene. "And what's your deal?" she asks her.

I frown and look down at my mate again. She doesn't say a word.

"Come on," Evo begins, taking Kenna's elbow from Bre and lifting her into his arms. "We'll discuss it inside." Evo starts walking before he halts and turns back to us. "Victoria, Jessup, Evalyn, I want you three to patrol. Any sound, anything suspicious and you sound the alarm. Got it?" The three of them, already naked, shift back to their wolves.

The rest of the pack follows Evo to the house through the vampire-dust-covered grass. The pack is lucky to suffer no casualties and, minus a few scrapes and bruises, no one was seriously injured.

Darla seems to have gotten the full brunt of the bruises. She's still fully naked and trying to cover her breasts with one hand and her nether regions with the other. She has a large bruise on her right shoulder, as well as several minor lacerations.

I step through the broken door, Irene behind me. I pull her along by her hand, unwilling to let her go. The glass crunches loudly underfoot.

Around the side of the kitchen, vines lay on the floor in a haphazard heap. The wood flooring is fractured from where the vines, now limp and brittle, seem to have come from.

My heart seizes in my chest. My mate was in here when this happened. She was in here, and I was out there . . .

I ignore the urge to protect my unharmed and safe mate and watch as Darla closes the fridge door before she scurries off. Kelsey is going to be so mad when she sees this.

"When is this shit going to end?" I comment in the living room minutes later. I take Irene to the couch and hold her hand until she sits on the cushion. She's in such a daze.

Kat sits next to her, placing an arm around her shoulder to comfort her friend.

Rubbing my head with both hands, I absentmindedly survey the room. The front door is wide open. I frown, move around the furniture, and approach it.

Grasping the handle, I begin to swing it shut. And then I stop. Something catches my eye, dim but sparkling in the moonlight. My eyebrows dip lower as I squint, curiosity taking over. I step out onto the porch, the wooden boards creaking under my weight.

Evo stops whatever he's saying and calls my name. "Everything okay?" he asks when I don't answer, but his words sound like they're coming from the end of a deep tunnel.

I take another step, the heap on the ground becoming more visible. My eyes pick out a shape attached to the large mass in the grass—a shoe. The design on the side is one I used to tease my best friend about.

I take another step and swallow thickly. I recognize the jeans, the shirt. And lastly, my eyes land on the glint caused by the moon . . .

Dead, unseeing eyes stare at the sky.

Thudding noises roar in my ear before I realize it's my heartbeat. My mouth is bone dry now, and my hands tingle as fear and adrenaline mix in my veins and puddle in my fingertips. My tongue sticks to the roof of my mouth and I blink several times, frantically trying to get rid of the scene in front of my eyes . . . as if this can't be real. But it is. It is real.

Reality hits and I fall to my knees with a thud in the grass next to the dead body.

My world breaks into pieces. My wolf silent with sorrow, stiff and disbelieving.

"Dyson," I whisper, my voice hoarse.

CHAPTER ELEVEN

Flint Rockland

I love you, man. Treat your mate right, okay? Don't waste a moment with her.

Those were Dyson's last words. The last words I'll ever hear him speak. His advice plays on constant repeat, his voice echoing over and over inside my head.

I watch his blank, unseeing eyes. My mind and wolf are in shock, unable to comprehend that our friend no longer exists. That though he's right there, laying on the grass, he's not actually there. All that's left is a hollow husk—a shell—of a life he once led . . . of the man he once was. He'll never speak again. I'll never hear his laugh again. He'll never breathe again. He'll never shift into his wolf again. He'll never . . .

A memory surfaces. In this memory, he fiddles with the setting on my computer, fixing what I broke. He turns his head and laughs at something I said. I was trying to reach his nerdy level, only to make a fool of myself. He called me out on it, like he always did, and we laughed it off together.

My heart shatters.

Evo rushes outside, his footsteps thundering in his haste. Darla, Kenna, Bre, Kat, and Irene follow right after him. Their scents swirl and mix with that of the dead body in front of me.

"Oh my God," Kenna whispers from behind me at the same time Kat says, "Holy shit."

"No. No. That's not . . . *N-No*," Bre whispers.

The crickets chirp to fill the silence around Evo's curses. The threat is gone and they feel safe enough to continue their song. If only the crickets knew that on this night, there's nothing to joyfully sing about.

Evo bends down on the other side of Dyson, rests his knees on the grass and runs a hand through his dark hair.

Dyson's body lays at an odd angle, limbs carelessly thrown about and his neck twisted awkwardly. It's like he was thrown . . . like he wasn't a person to whoever put him there, but instead, a burden of flesh. Trash to be discarded.

Grief and sorrow swell in my chest as my eyes flick to the rope marks around Dyson's neck.

"They tied him up and hung him," Evo whispers. He carefully picks up one of Dyson's wrists and examines the bruises.

"Who did this?" Bre asks. She sobs with a slight hiccup.

"The vampires?" Kenna asks, her voice muffled by the hand over her mouth.

Irene places her hand on my back, her rubbing motion too stiff to be soothing.

Irene Scott

Internally, I panic at Bre's question. I know exactly who did it and why.

You'll regret this. That's what Jazz said before I left. I distinctly remember the sneer on her face.

You know, Irene. You're not the only spy we have. You are disposable, she had said.

The word 'disposable' echoes in my head. Dyson . . . Dyson was their—

"You okay?" Kenna asks. I glance up. She's rubbing her belly, feeling my inner turmoil and directing her question at me with concern.

"It's just a lot," I mumble, averting my gaze.

Unfortunately, the only place to look is at Dyson's body. People look so different when they're dead. The stress of their life and thoughts are no longer evident on their face. It makes them seem younger and haunting at the same time.

This is my fault. I did this. I didn't obey and now this pack is paying the price, one life at a time.

"What kind of grudge do the vampires hold against your pack?" Kat asks.

Evo stands from Dyson's body and runs a hand down his face. "I don't know. Ben and Romaine are waiting for me before they start questioning the hostage. I'm sure we'll find out."

Kat squints as she considers something. "It's against the rules, but since I no longer belong to a coven . . . Rules be damned."

I frown before my head snaps to her, her words catching me off guard. I didn't know she was no longer a part of her coven. I just talked to her yesterday and she never mentioned it.

Taking a step forward toward Dyson's body, Kat takes a deep breath and closes her eyes. The pack watches her as she begins mumbling something I don't understand.

The crickets continue their chirp, the vibrations mingling with the sound of tiny rocks clinking together by the gravel driveway. I glance in the direction and see several pebbles bouncing and hopping in the grass, heading our way. When they reach Dyson, they begin assembling themselves, creating a picture in the grass. The clinking stops when the picture is complete, a face taking shape.

My knees buckle when I recognize the face.

Zane. It's a face I'd never forget.

"Who is that?" Kenna asks, craning her neck to see the face better. Tears stream down her rosy cheeks.

"Zane," Darla growls.

Brenna points. "That's one of the guys who attacked me in the parking garage last year."

Evo frowns. "Who's Zane?"

Darla's eyes glow, her anger getting the better of her and riling her wolf. "He'd arrive as Jazz's entourage when they'd visit George. A man of few words, but one I never wanted to mess with."

Evo stuffs his hands into his pockets and a flash of green takes over his irises. Reality seems to set in for him, as it does for me. We're all in danger. If I'm not careful, they'll discover what I am before I have a chance to work out my next plan.

"This is Jazz's rogue posse?" he growls.

Darla nods. "She has many behind her, fawning over her every step." She shakes her head. "I don't understand it myself."

"When will she just leave us alone?" Bre spits. She wipes her eyes roughly with the heel of her palm.

Kenna snarls, her face hardening. "I'm fucking done with that bitch." She whirls and begins stomping her way to the house. It is more of a waddle with heavy footfalls. "If I have to do this myself, I'll make sure that girl is sent straight to the flames of hell. She can take it up with the devil himself."

I need to think of something. No . . . I have to *do* something. No more deaths will fall on my shoulders. If I pass over that baby, this won't be the pack's only death. Jazz will stop at nothing to ruin their lives. And with this revolution, I start to form the plan that I should have from the beginning.

Kenna takes a step up on the stairs and stops.

"Kenna?" Evo asks after a moment.

Kenna looks down at the wetness spreading down her legs. "I– I think I just peed myself."

"Shit," I curse. My heart drops into my stomach. *Of course*. Of course, this would happen now! "Bre, call Jacob and have him send Reese."

Bre pulls her phone from her pocket, her fingers quickly swiping across the surface. She places the phone to her ear.

Evo rushes over to Kenna's side, the rest of the pack—except Flint, who is still wordlessly staring at Dyson—follows him, confused expressions on their faces. Evo looks at the wetness forming around Kenna's nightgown. "What's happening? What's going on?" he asks me from over his shoulder.

"Her water broke," I say numbly. I leave Flint's side and help Kenna up the next two steps and across the porch. We stop at the door frame and she grabs the door handle. Her jaw tightens and she bends, pain filling her eyes with fresh tears.

"Holy shit," Kenna grunts, clutching her stomach.

"Is that a contraction?" Bre pockets her phone and dashes to her side. Her voice is less excited than a normal 'aunt-to-be' would be. The death of a pack mate is taking this cherishing moment right out from under them. And it's my fault.

"Yes," I say patiently as I wait for Kenna to stand upright.

Darla squeezes past us and points to the stairs. "To their bedroom?"

I nod and she crosses the living room to take hurried steps up the stairs to prep. She's had two kids of her own—I have faith that she knows what she is doing.

Kat taps me on the shoulder. "I'm going to head home," she mumbles.

"Can you wait? For just a minute?" I ask, and Kat reluctantly agrees while crossing her arms over her chest. I turn to Evo. "Will you carry her up the stairs? Bre, can you help Darla?"

Both dutifully take on their tasks in stride and disappear. I peek outside the door. Flint is now holding Dyson's hand. My heart breaks for him and the pack, but I have a plan that needs to be implemented. Jazz won't stop until she gets what she wants.

I fold Kat's hand into my own and lead her to the kitchen. I suddenly stop by the island and whirl on her. She nearly knocks into me. "What are you?" I demand.

She frowns. "What do you mean?"

I swat the air between us. "Kat . . . I've never seen a witch with such strong capabilities. And your eyes had a fiery ring around the rims." I mimic a circular motion around my irises. "And you had a ball of flames in your hand!"

She remains silent, chewing on the inside of her lip.

I take a deep breath, trying to ease my tense tone. "Is this why you no longer have a coven?"

She shrugs, her teeth freeing her lip. "Yes. But I can't talk about it. Not right now."

I growl as I search her eyes. Her sincerity pleads with me to understand. I sigh, slump my shoulders, and rub at my neck. Eventually, I nod. Secrets people can't discuss is something I'm privy to. Except, this time, I'm going to share my secret with her . . . because I have no choice.

I did this. It's my job to make it right. It may be my brother's life on the line, but my choice is simple. Sacrifice one and save many, or save the one and doom many. In the light of day, at this very moment, the choice is clear . . . and I may not survive it. That's something I can live with. Peace for this pack is something I can live with. Or die with . . .

"I need your help," I declare, my words rushing out of my mouth. Time is precious.

Flint Rockland

Sliding the back of my hands across the blades of grass, I push them under Dyson's body, curl my arms underneath him, and lift. His head falls back at an odd angle and his mouth hangs agape as his lifeless eyes continue to watch the sky.

I stare at him. The breeze brushes at my wet cheeks, and I take the steps up the porch and enter the house. Smells, lights, textures, and sounds seem more surreal than they were before.

I head to the last remaining guest room just off the living room and gently place him on the bed. Hushed voices can be heard throughout the house, along with Kenna's groans from upstairs. I block the sounds out, my focus on my lost friend.

My friend, my pack mate . . .

My wolf grieves inside me, howls until his cry of pain momentarily replaces my thoughts. I cross Dyson's arms over his chest and sob as I close his eyes with shaky fingers.

"I love you, too, man," I whisper. The lump in my throat makes my voice harsh.

I stare at him for seconds. Minutes. Hours? The front door closes, taking me from my memories. I exit the room and wipe my face with the bottom of my shirt.

Taking a deep breath, I search for my alphas and climb the stairs to where I know they'll both be. My footsteps are loud in such a quiet house. The chatter from the kitchen is gone, but I can hear Kenna curse from their bedroom. I figure Irene will be in there, tending to Kenna's needs. I need my mate, even if she's busy. Her presence will be enough.

I knock on their bedroom door and enter without an invitation. Darla is holding Kenna's hand while Evo sits behind her on the bed, his hands rubbing her lower back.

Bre walks over to me, fresh tears staining her blushed cheeks, and gives me a hug. Kenna's hair whips out of her sweaty face as she glares at the door. "Where's Irene?" she growls.

I frown and glance around the room. "She's not here?"

Sniffling, Bre steps away from me, her scowl distorting her features. "She told me to call Jacob for Reese, which I did, but I haven't seen her since. I thought she was downstairs with you and . . ." her voice trails off as her eyes slide to the floor. Her grief is thick in the air, like the gale of a storm. A tear slips down her cheek, drips from her jaw, and splats against the floor.

I shake my head, swallowing the lump in my throat. "She's not downstairs."

"Never mind that," Evo says. "She'll turn up—she probably needed a breather. It's been a bad day for everyone."

"We seem to be a fucking lightning rod for those," Kenna barks.

Evo glances at her before returning his eyes to mine. "Ben and Romaine are starting the interrogation. Would you mind assisting them?"

I nod once. The vampires brought my dead friend to our doorstep, and it's time to return the favor.

Anger replaces my sorrow. I march from the alphas' quarters and back into the quiet night. The dew is setting in and it's slick like blood beneath my shoes. A stick snaps under my foot as I make my way to the garage with purpose in my step.

In front of the garage's side door, I wipe my face with the palm of my hand before I place it on the handle. I pause, hearing the crunch of gravel just as Reese's car pulls into the driveway. Lingering by the door for a moment, I point my finger to the main house when she waves at me. She gives a curt nod and climbs out of her car, still wearing her scrubs from work.

I step inside the garage, the dim light comforting to my swollen eyes. Ben, Romaine, and the vampire turn their attention to me as I enter, my shoes padding softly across the cement. On the way, I glance at the car Irene and I drove in for our date— a happier, less complicated time.

The rage I felt earlier returns swiftly, and I refocus my attention on the vampire. Black veins are visible under his skin. His eyes are as red as the blood he drinks. But, other than that . . . he looks . . . civil. His pointed fangs seem less threatening when he doesn't hiss, and his intelligent gaze studies every part of me – every subtle twitch I make.

My eyes travel down to his folded hands in his lap. "Why the hell isn't he shackled?" I growl.

Ben and Romaine, who sit in lawn chairs across from him, stand up. Ben holds his hand out. "He's not a threat. He's willing to give information." Ben frowns as he takes me in. "What happened to you?"

I stop just in front of him. "Dyson is dead."

His frown falls. "What happened?" he barks.

"Your little vampire friends dropped him on the doorstep," I say to the vampire in the chair.

The vampire's throat bobs. Ben whirls to vampire, and the vampire holds up his hands, palms facing us. "Let me explain."

"You better get to it," Ben growls, his fist clenching at his sides.

The vampire's red eyes wildly flit between us. "She killed him."

Romaine grabs his shirt by the collar and yanks him up. A stirring of his stench reaches my nose – the stench of death and rot. "Who is she?"

"The One."

Ben balls his fists into a tighter knot, the knuckles white. "I'm so sick of hearing about someone who calls themselves The One. Who is this person?"

The vampire stutters, then finally spits out words. "I don't know her name. She called on us. Paid us a wealthy fee to stop by here . . ." his voice trails off and he visually traces a tire. "She's going to be so mad when I'm the only one to return."

'Paid a wealthy fee,' echoes in my head. The money in the safe . . .

If I have anything to say about it, he won't be leaving the spot he stands on.

"What does she look like?" I ask, the anger barely contained in my voice as my eyes glow. I already know the answer.

"I only saw her once. Blonde hair, huge shoes, loads of sparkly crap on her wrists."

Romaine cocks his head. "You mean jewelry?"

The vampire bobs his head and Romaine shoves him back into the seat before turning to Ben and me. "She used to visit the Gray Pack."

"It's Jazz," I mumble.

Ben gives a curt nod. "I have no doubt."

I turn back to the vampire. "Why did the rogues kill Dyson?"

The vampire scowls, as if we should have already suspected the answer. "Because he was of no use to her anymore."

My nails dig into my palms. "What do you mean?"

He shrugs. "I wasn't informed."

Then it hits me, and I stumble back a step. Dyson's last words repeat in my head as Ben growls and demands more answers from the vampire. Their voices sound muffled, like they are underwater, while I revisit the memory again.

I love you, man. Treat your mate right, okay? Don't waste a moment with her.

"He was saying goodbye," I whisper, staring over the top of the vampire's head and seeing nothing but Dyson walking off to the garage for his errand.

Three sets of eyes land on me.

"What?" Romaine asks.

"Dyson. The last thing he said to me. I thought it was odd at the time . . . but he was saying goodbye."

Ben frowns. "How could he possibly know he was going to die tonight?"

The vampire purses his lips over his fangs. "Perhaps your friend was a double crosser."

The three of us remain silent. More information pops into my head.

After George broke my leg, my wolf shifted, and they separated us. In my absence, did Dyson compromise with George? Did he agree to help him? So that the two of us would live?

Dyson's hygiene had declined since I was able to shift back. He avoided the pack. His voice breaks into my head—memories of the past weeks.

I was trying to keep you alive.

Just remember, Flint, you're not the only one who suffers.

Not a whole lot. Research. A lot of video games, I guess. Trying to get right with myself.

Actually, I have an errand to run, but I'll be back.

I love you, man.

"He did it to save my life." I scrub my face and plop into a lawn chair, disgusted with myself.

I don't know what sort of information he was feeding Jazz, but he saved my life, and in the end, sacrificed his own.

Ben puts a comforting hand on my shoulder and squeezes. "That's not all we've discovered tonight, Flint."

I glance up at him.

He continues with reluctance, "Our little friend here," he nods at the vampire, "said your mate has been a busy girl. One of his own was ordered to deliver a message. A message to do as she's told, or our pack falls."

The vampire shakes his head. "No, no, no. That wasn't the message. It was, 'bring the baby or the pack dies.'" He narrows his red eyes at Ben.

My heart skips a beat, denial thick in my veins as it continues to pump. "No." I shake my head. "Irene wouldn't be teaming up with Jazz."

The vampire giggles. "Oh, but she would. She did. She has."

I stare at him. The sounds of voices are once again blocked out. My jaw ticks, but the rest of my face remains relaxed like it's unable to decide which emotions I should display first. I ball my fist as my claw expands, and my eyes glow to their own accord. Ben calls my name in a warning, but I don't listen.

Quick as a flash, I bury my clawed fingers into his chest, the sound like a boom of thunder as it breaks through skin and bone. The vampire's giggle is cut off and his eyes widen. It feels just like the last heart—thick, slimy, heavy. I squish his heart, and when I pull it out, he dusts on the chair.

I stare at the pile of all that's left of him, hear the garage clock tick the seconds by. Every feeling I have is raw and exposed. I refuse to back down from these feelings, refuse to shove it down like I would have in the past. Dyson deserves these feelings. He deserves to be grieved, and despite it all, he deserves justice.

"You going to be okay, Flint?" Romaine asks softly. He bends beside the chair and tries to make eye contact. I don't answer.

"Where's Irene?" Ben mumbles angrily.

My own mate betrayed me.

CHAPTER TWELVE

Irene Scott

I park my car where the greasy blond, Luke, always parked. Funny—twice before, I was a hostage. Now, I'm a willing victim, sacrificing my life, and possibly my brother's, in an effort to save my mate, his pack, and the newborn that will surely soon arrive.

The territory wasn't hard to find. A quick peek inside Dyson's quarters and the information was instilled in my brain, frozen, like a map burned behind my eyelids.

Before, I worried about Flint dying. I worried about my new friends. I worried about my brother. I never thought I'd be the one to succumb to that fate.

I take the keys from the ignition and jingle them in my hand. What do I do with them? I suppose it doesn't matter. Nothing matters but putting one foot in front of the other. Nothing matters but getting this over with. And in this moment, as I stand by my car clutching my keys while knowing what I must do, I internally exist where time has more meaning. I exist in a place where decisions have weight, and every nerve in my body is alive and ripe with the choice I've chosen. This deal with Jazz began with me, and it will end with me.

Irene? Jacob growls in my head. *Where are you? Ben just called and said you've gone off the radar. They're trying to find you.*

I close my eyes and sag my shoulders. I had been hoping I wouldn't have to say goodbye to anyone. I had hoped that I could have a sliver of dignity once I died.

Irene? Jacob tries again, a little softer. *If you're in trouble, you need to tell me.*

With a long and drawn out exhale, I sever my link to my pack. Inside my head, an invisible band snaps, ending the connection to my alpha . . . to my loved ones . . . to my friends. My wolf stills inside me, the disconnect painful for her. She howls inside me, angry with my choice and this situation. She has no pack. We have no pack. But it doesn't matter. Not for much longer.

I place my keys in the cup holder, climb out, and shut my car door.

A swarm of rogue wolves exit the shed like an army of ants, and I step away from my car.

Naturally, Zane reaches me first. He grips my arm, twists it behind my back, and slams me into the side of my car. I wince at the pain to my face—a bruise will surely form there.

Jazz comes into my view, her scowl matching those around her. She stops and stares at me with her manicured nails on her narrow hips. "Go. Make sure she's alone," she says to no one in particular. Several wolves melt away and jog off to investigate.

"I'm alone," I try to tell her.

"Sure, you are." She crosses her arms, a smirk replacing her scowl. "Did you get my little present?"

My eyes glow wolf. "The dead pack mate or the hoard of vampires? You'll have to be more specific because both were surprise-worthy."

She waves a hand in the air. "The dead wolf, of course. The vampires were just for fun. I had to get the dead body on the territory without detection, you know."

I growl, my bruised cheek vibrating against the metal of the car. How can this woman have no feelings about the man she just killed – about the man who used to be her pack mate? "Mission accomplished."

She giggles like a teenager whose daddy just bought her a brand-new car. "Good." She looks inside my car. "Where's the baby?"

"Not here."

Jazz clucks her tongue. "That's unfortunate. Before dear Dyson lost his life, he shared some information. I should be congratulating you on finding your mate. But . . . that sort of acknowledgment would hold no meaning coming from me."

I flex my jaw in answer. "Don't you dare touch Flint."

Jazz continues, her voice so sickly sweet it raises goosebumps on my arms, "I don't think we'll need that baby, after all."

I glare, my eyes still glowing wolf and reflecting off the paint of my car.

She leans against the car and gazes at the stars. "Now that we have you, the mate to a Cloven Pack member, they'll surely come for you." Her gaze turns deadly before her eyes lower to mine. "I don't plan to let you live long enough to witness it," she adds, each word clipped and dipped with malicious intent.

She nods her head at Zane. He yanks me from the car and shoves me toward the shed, my fate in his hands.

Flint Rockland

Ben hangs up the phone on the way back to the house. "Jacob said she severed herself from their pack."

I stop dead in my tracks, my heart pounding, my wolf terrified. "What does that mean?"

"It means we have limited time to find her. She ran, Flint. She's gone rogue. If she's out there, roaming the streets with no place to go, no pack, it won't take long before insanity kicks in."

Romaine, Ben, and I ascend the stairs to the porch and find Kat waiting on a lawn chair. Rage rips through my body at the sight of her, but she pays no mind to my shaky frame.

She steps into our path. "I need to talk to you guys."

"Not now, witch," I snarl. "We're busy." I move to walk past her. She steps in my way again.

"It's about Irene," she says with confidence.

"What about her?"

"She was blackmailed by someone named Jazz."

"What?" Ben barks.

"Look, she told me she had no choice but to play spy. They have her brother."

My face relaxes, realization cooling my heated temperature. I remember her talking about her brother with adoration, and then she quickly skipped the rest of the topic. That's what she was hiding. That was what I was foolish enough to dismiss.

Why isn't anyone who they say they are anymore? Why does everything come with layers of secrets and deceit?

"Where is she?" I demand.

Kat hesitates as all three of our eyes glow. She pulls at the bottom of her shirt, nervous to reveal information to three angry shifters.

"She went to Jazz," she mumbles.

"Why the fuck would she do that?" I yell.

Kat flinches. "She was told to bring the baby in exchange for her brother. After Dyson was left dead on your doorstep, she made a plan—to offer herself in exchange for the baby."

"She's sacrificing herself and her brother?" Romaine asks, disbelief in his voice.

Kat nods. "You can't let her. You have to go after her."

I rake a hand through my hair and begin pacing the deck. A war happens inside me. A war between betrayal and knowing she's trying to fix it . . . *on her own*.

Shit!

Why didn't she come to me? Why didn't she tell me anything? I need to do something—I have to do something. That's my mate. Our mating hasn't progressed enough that if she died, I would die, but that's of no matter. I won't let her sacrifice herself, even if she kept all this from me and . . . I won't let her die.

Evo steps outside. "What's going on? Is the interrogation done?"

Ben tells him everything, starting with what the vampire said, to the double crossing of Irene. Then Kat tells him her side of the story. When they're finished, Evo grabs his hair before dropping his hands to his sides. He thinks for a moment, his jaw ticking. "This night just gets better and better," he says sarcastically. He stretches his neck, stress lines wrinkle his forehead, and he glances up at me. "Flint . . ." I stop my pacing and reluctantly look at my alpha. "Any idea how to find your mate?"

I raise my eyebrows, shocked at his question. I thought Evo would want to destroy her once he found out. The shock wears off, allowing me to think for a moment. Dyson would know – he'd know what to do next. But he's dead. Dead people can't talk. Dead people can't hijack a phone's location.

"Can you conjure the dead?" I ask Kat. "The shades or whatever you call them from wherever you said they're at."

She shakes her head. "Anything against the natural order—death or dying—is against the rules. It has some serious repercussions. You don't mess with the realms, the Fee, and their order."

"Fuck," I growl. Ben places a hand on my shoulder. "Dyson said something about research. What was he researching?"

Evo frowns. "I have no idea. I was giving him space to deal with his . . . you know." He clears his throat. "I didn't know he was working on anything."

The silence stretches on as we take a moment to breathe deeply and come up with a solution. It's obvious in the way everyone stands that the mention of Dyson's names cuts fresh wounds into our hearts.

"Maybe he has something in his quarters?" Kat whispers, shrugging when we glance at her.

Romaine blows out a breath. "It's worth a shot."

The thought of going inside his quarters, seeing evidence of Dyson's life, causes me to take pause. An internal war shifts inside me again, a tornado of emotions and reluctance. I shove it aside and take action.

I descend the steps two at a time and head toward Dyson's quarters with a determined march. Everyone, including Kat, follows along, but when I place my hand on the doorknob, I hesitate. My hand curls around it and grips it with more force than necessary.

Ben places his hand over mine. "Together," he suggests quietly.

I nod, letting him know I appreciate it, and we open the door together.

One by one, we file slowly into his quarters, dumbstruck at what we see. Lining the walls are hand drawn and computer animated maps. News clippings from unexplained malicious dog attacks, robberies, pictures of people who once belonged to a pack, are all tacked or taped to the walls.

I examine a name and face I recognize from earlier. The picture has Dyson's handwriting scribbled across the bottom of it. In red permanent ink, it says *Zane Michaels*. The picture is pinned next to Zane's information: Rogue, once a member of the Bane Pack. Banned for treachery.

I've heard the rumors about the Bane Pack. They're treacherous, dangerous, and if this man was banned from that pack . . .

I continue down the line of pictures. Several of them and their descriptions are pinned to this wall.

Ben stands behind me and glances at Zane's picture. "That's one of the guys who attacked Bre."

"He's also the guy who killed Dyson," I mumble. I vow for him to be the first to go. My wolf growls in agreement.

I step over to the other wall—the one Evo and Kat study that's full of maps and locations. Feeling me coming up behind him, Evo nods toward the map he's studying, labeled 'The Castle.'

"This isn't too far from here," he says, tapping the map.

"They've been under our noses the whole time," I mumble.

Evo rakes a hand through his hair. "And he knew the whole time."

"Yeah." I stuff my hands into my pockets.

"Guys," Romaine calls. We turn to face him, and he waves around a piece of paper. "He left a note."

I stride over to him and snatch the note, my eyes flitting over the familiar hand script.

Flint,

If you're reading this, I'm already gone. I made a terrible mistake, and for that, I apologize.

During captivity, I made a deal with George. In exchange for your life, I offered my servitude—to report back to him about our pack. At the time, I believed I didn't have a choice. But I did. There's always a choice, and I realize that I made the wrong one.

After George died, I thought I was free. But I wasn't. Jazz found me, claimed that the favor was now hers. Since she and George were a team, I was now her unwilling servant.

I plan to go to her tonight. To do what I should have done with George. Should I not live, I hope you can forgive me for all I've done.

Dyson

I hold the note in shaky hands, rereading the words before Evo takes the note and reads it for himself.

"Fuck," he growls. "Why the hell is everything going to shit!" He passes the note to Ben before pacing back and forth in a short line, his hands on his hips. After a moment, he grumbles, "I've got to go, Kenna is calling me. Ben, let me know the plan when you have one."

Ben nods absentmindedly, and Evo makes his way out of Dyson's quarters.

Kat rocks on her heels, her hands stuffed into the back pockets of her jeans. "So, what is the plan?"

Ben sighs. "Flint." I glance at him. "Call the Riva Pack. Romaine, gather our wolves—leave two behind to help guard Evo and Kenna."

Kat asks again, a little impatient, "What's the plan, guys?"

I glance at her. "We're going to storm the fucking Castle and burn it to the ground."

"Does this mean you're coming with?" Ben asks her. "We could use . . . whatever magic you're using."

Biting the inside of her cheek, she hesitates. I answer for her. "No, she can't. Witches don't stick their noses in pack business, and should things go wrong —"

"The rogue pack would go after her, and her coven," Ben finishes. He exhales. "You should go, but Kat?"

"Hmm," she says distractedly.

"Thank you for helping today."

She nods and starts to walk away. A few feet away, she slowly comes to a halt, and says over her shoulder, "Please, save her."

CHAPTER THIRTEEN

Irene Scott

They take me out back, purposefully dragging me along so my feet can't keep up. I keep my eyes on the ground while trying to maintain my balance.

"Irene?" a voice croaks in horror.

I glance up, searching for the familiar voice, and find a man tied to a tree. My heart seizes in my chest. "Drake!" I yell.

Zane yanks me, wordlessly telling me to shut up. I struggle against his grip despite his warning.

"Are you okay?" I ask as they tie me to the tree next to him.

He doesn't answer. His protruding bones let me know that they haven't been feeding him. Dark circles squat under his eyes, and fresh and old bruises riddle his exposed skin. Wearing ripped and dirty clothes, the smell that comes from him would have wrinkled my nose on a normal day. But today isn't normal, and there's no reason to bathe a dead man walking.

Zane cinches the rope too tight and I hiss in pain.

"Don't hurt her!" Drake yells, fighting against his ropes weakly. His eyes flicker green.

A tear falls down my face, the reality of this choice setting in. The wolves step back, Luke grinning like a fool. With a hand smudged with dirt, he holds a large stick with fire lit on the end.

I turn back to my brother. "I love you," I tell him, because that's all the comfort I can give.

His eyes narrow at the torch. "What are you doing here? You should have run," he growls to me. "You should have never come back."

"It's more complicated than that." Another tear streams down my face.

The reflecting light from the flaming torch dances across his skin as Luke draws closer. Luke giggles hysterically, like a cackling hyena, and slowly lowers the flaming torch to Drake's leg. Drake stiffens as he tries to hold his ground, but he can't hold back the scream when the flames singe the hairs. The smell of burning flesh reaches my nose and panic makes my heart skip a beat.

"Stop!" I yell, fighting against my ropes. Drakes screams ricochet against the trees. "Stop it!"

Luke lifts the flame from his skin and my brother's screams quiet to whimpers. Luke glances at me, a smile spreading across his face as the rogue members watch with raptured interest.

He heads my direction, intent on the same assault. I lean as far away from him as I can when his breath fans across my cheek.

"Such a pretty little thing." He licks my cheek and I recoil. My eyes glow, a stubborn warning.

He lowers the flame. "Please, no." I shake my head back and forth. "Please, don't."

Drake yells at him, repeating the same words that are coming out of my mouth. Jazz makes her way through the crowd. Zane follows her with a gas can, the contents sloshing around inside. "Enough, Luke. Your fun will come."

Luke hesitates for a moment, his smile disappearing as he contemplates his order. Finally, he steps back. The breath I've been holding is released, and new, blessed air reaches my lungs.

Makenna Goldwin

I groan when another contraction hits. Evo massages my back while I stand by the bed and lean into the mattress. The pain throbs in waves of heat and it takes everything I have not to scream a stream of curses.

The contraction relaxes and I rock back and forth, still leaning on the bed. "I need drugs. Lots and lots of drugs," I say into the duvet.

Reese glances at me at the same time I look at her. "You're too late for drugs."

I wipe my hair out of my sweaty face. "Are you fucking kidding me?"

Reese puckers her lips, having heard it all in her line of work. "You've passed that mark, honey." She pats the bed. "Here, lay down. Let me confirm."

My mom and Evo help me onto the bed. Bre disappeared a while ago, and I haven't seen Irene since I came to my room. It's nearing dawn already, and no one seems to be around.

Reese slides her fingers in and checks my cervix. "Yep, I feel the hair. No drugs."

I groan as another contraction hits. Reese checks her watch.

"It's okay, baby," Evo murmurs, combing his fingers through my hair. He continues to coo, and I flop my head back on the pillow and glare at the texture of the ceiling.

Sweat trickles down every slope of my body and my nightgown sticks like a second layer of skin.

"Oh, you shut your mouth!" I yell eventually yell at him. "This baby is ripping out of me, Evo. And you're keeping things from me. I may be pushing a watermelon from a teeny, tiny hole, but that doesn't make me oblivious." I grunt, pain in my lower back rippling up my spine. "And my best friend isn't here. My midwife is off the radar." I glance at Reese. "I feel like I need to push. Should I push?"

Reese lifts my nightgown again. "Oh, wow."

"Oh, wow?" I snarl. "Oh, wow? That's your professional assessment?"

She ignores me. "Okay honey, on your next contraction, I want you to push, okay?"

Oh, shit. I turn pleading eyes to Evo. I'm not ready for this. I'm not ready!

"You're almost done," he says, grinning. "The baby is almost here. You can do this."

I grip the sheets, feeling the beginning of my stomach muscles tighten. I moan—a deep moan that sounds foreign to my own ears—and push as instructed. Squeezing Evo and my mom's hands with all my strength, a scream rips from my throat.

Flint Rockland

We pull into the gravel road and park our two cars a mile from our destination. I throw the map on the dashboard and peer out the window. Forest surrounds the road and weeds crawl across the rocks. There are no streetlamps here—the only thing lighting the landscape is the moon and stars.

Ben, Romaine, Bre, Victoria, Jessup, Evalyn, and I climb out of the cars, our feet crunching on gravel. I slam my door shut and begin pacing with my hands on my hips. We could be out of time. We could be out of time and she'll be just as dead as . . .

"We'll get her, Flint," Bre says, attempting to comfort me.

I whip around to face her. "Before they kill her?" I growl. "Or after they torture her?"

She looks away from me and remains silent. She can't guarantee either of these things and she knows it.

"The Riva Pack should be here any minute," Ben comments, checking his watch.

Silence stretches between everyone. The only noise are the birds as they chirp in the trees, awake and already searching for their meals. We'll be entering those trees, leading us straight to Jazz and her band of fucking assholes.

My wolf paces inside me, mimicking my own actions.

Headlights flick across the road and over our clothes. I breathe a sigh of relief as the Riva Pack pulls up behind our cars. I begin walking toward the first car, anxious to get this going.

Jacob exits quickly with a fierce expression, along with his beta, Rex. "Thanks for calling," Jacob begins. "Where are they?"

Ben jogs up to my side and points into the shadows of the trees. "That way, about a mile. We'll be walking from here."

Rex and Jacob nod. The other Riva shifters exit their cars and begin to wordlessly undress.

Ben continues, "These are rogue wolves we're dealing with. They'll fight dirty, and most likely have weapons. The goal here is to retrieve Irene and her brother."

"And to kill as many of the fuckers as you can," I add.

CHAPTER FOURTEEN

Irene Scott

I watch, fidgeting with my ropes again, as they pour gasoline over my brother. He squirms against the tree, trying to get away from the offending and destructive liquid.

Examining a fingernail, Jazz backs away from the splash of the gasoline. The rogues around her chat with each other, like this is some social gathering and not an execution. My wolf snorts in disgust. They have no sympathy for their own kind, not a drop of humanity left in them.

Zane checks the binds around our wrists again, making sure they are secure, while Luke travels in my direction with the gas can. "Time to burn that pretty skin of yours, little lady. It's a real shame. I could lick every inch of you, maybe take a bite or two. A real beauty." He licks his lips, giggles, and then lifts the can.

A few drops drip on my skin, the smell burning my nose and eyes. I open my mouth to spit on his face, but a howl sounds in the distance.

My heart leaps in my chest.

All the rogue wolves and I glance toward the woods where the sound came from. Luke pauses his pouring, lowering the can down to his side.

"What was that?" someone asks in the crowd.

"Is anyone on patrol?" another asks.

"You're an idiot," someone answers. "We don't have anyone on patrol. We're all here, you fool!"

"Zane," Jazz warns, and before she can say anything else, more howls follow the first.

Hope blooms in my chest before I squash it. Hope is a dangerous thing. It can suck you into its depths with such promise before it shatters before your eyes.

"Light the fire!" Jazz yells. She slices a hand through the air. "Like the damn fire!"

Luke drops the can of gas. The lit torch is still in his other hand, and he scrambles back to my brother with it.

Drake pleads unintelligible words as I cry. "No. No! You can't! Leave him alone!" I fight against my ropes with all my strength. I vaguely think to shift, but I know in the position I'm in, it'll do more harm than good. The ropes would break my wolf's bones, rendering me useless to help my brother.

Luke touches the fire to my brother's skin and he's immediately engulfed in bright orange flames.

"Drake!" I yell. His screams erupt into the night. The sound is inhuman, thick, and full of an unimaginable agony. "Drake!"

Flint Rockland

Some of us are partially shifted while others are in full wolf form. We race through the trees toward the rogues, weaving between trunks and hopping over boulders. Low hanging tree branches snap against my arms, face, and torso.

From the adrenaline, many of our entourage howls as they race, echoing through the trees and encouraging me to move faster, faster, *faster*. My lungs burn and the smell of burning flesh soon reaches my nose. This tells me two things: One, we are close. Two, they're burning a body. The stench is unmistakable.

My wolf and I panic, frightened that it's our mate. The probability is high for such a scenario.

I squint in the woods as I pump my arms. In the distance, I hear a ruckus in the woods, and soon, running rogue shifters – some partially shifted, some fully shifted – barrel toward us. Snarls and growls break through as they clash with our group.

The first to engage is Ben and Bre—the leaders of our group. Ben grabs the first wolf and throws him, slamming him into a nearby tree. I barely avoid the hurling body, but I keep pushing forward.

"Keep going!" Ben hollers to both Bre and myself.

I push harder, passing Bre. Ben shoulders his way into a running rogue and the rogue flips, rumbling in the forest brush. And soon, I'm outrunning him.

Ahead, a partially shifted wolf steps in my path. The male with blond hair giggles as he stalks closer. The sound escaping his mouth is distorted by his canines. I slow to a walk and take a stalking step toward him, intent to destroy.

A blur of dark fur barrels into the partially shifted wolf, knocking both of them to the ground. Snarls and teeth clashing vibrate in my ears. The wolf is Jacob, his scent reaching my nose as the breeze shifts.

I veer around them and continue forward at a run until I reach the end of the tree line. The battle noises behind me sing through the night. Screams of pain, howls, growls, curses—I leave it behind as I advance out of the woods.

I halt in a small clearing at the side of a large shed. My eyes zoom in on the blaze that has a whole tree lit on fire.

Jazz's back is turned to me, but relief fills me. She's talking to my mate not far from the burning tree. She's alive. *Irene is alive.*

I glare at the back of Jazz's head. Her long, platinum hair is flat as a board, even with the slight breeze. A large man is beside her. *Zane.* He turns toward me as soon he hears my feet rustle against the grass.

I continue advancing, intent on getting to my mate and mowing down the bastard who is going to step in my way. A sneer contorts his lips, and he marches toward me with balled-up fists.

Irene Scott

My heart fills with relief when Flint steps from the trees, and instantly sinks when Zane stalks toward him.

They rush toward each other, and Flint punches Zane in the jaw with a quick strike. Jazz turns her back on me as soon as Zane grunts his pain. I blink several times, attempting to get the tears to clear from my face.

My brother is dead. Burned to nothing. And now my mate . . .

I take the moment to try wiggling through my ropes again, but they're too tight. I need to get out of here. I need to help. I need to be something more than a helpless fool stuck to a damn tree!

Zane throws his fist at Flint, but Flint slaps it away like a fly. His clawed hand scrapes Zane's wrist as he does so. For a moment, for a single breath, Zane glances at his bleeding wrist. He roars and partially shifts, and as he does, Jazz crosses her arms. I imagine her grinning, believing Zane will outmatch Flint.

The two begin to circle each other, their bodies slightly crouched, ready to spring. Zane charges and Flint kicks out his foot, connecting to Zane and sending him tumbling to the ground. Zane flips himself from his back to his feet and swipes his claws out. Flint isn't prepared this time and receives three large gashes across his chest. Blood immediately seeps down his shirt.

No, no, no!

Brenna Johnson

I place my clawed hands around her head—one at the base and one at the jaw—of the partially shifted wolf. She's on her knees before me, forced there by a well-aimed kick to her knee cap. Her leg had snapped on impact.

As she continues to howl in pain, I twist her head with all my strength. The snapping of her spine vibrates in my clawed fingertips, and her cries of pain are cut off. I let go of her head and she drops to the ground. Lifeless. *Dead.*

Instead of staring at the body like I want to, I glance around. If I stare, I'll think about it. If I think about it, awareness will click. I've just ended a life. That should never sit right with anyone. Rogue life or not, she was still a living being.

I shove the thoughts aside before they consume me.

Ben is engaged with a wolf who's fully shifted. The wolf charges at him, snarling and snapping his jaw. Ben punches him between the eyes. At this close of proximity, the sound of the hit is quite loud.

Startled, the wolf shakes his head with a whine, trying to gain back his vision. Ben takes the opportunity, grips the wolf's fur, and slams the wolf onto the ground. He straddles him and curls his hands around his fur-covered throat. The wolf attempts to snap his teeth at Ben's exposed arms, his front claws raking against Ben's chest.

I wince, my heart thudding in slight fear for my mate. Blood oozes from his fresh cuts. Through our mating, I can feel Ben's pain, but he continues strangling the wolf, undistracted. He's in his dark place, completing his tasks in a detached frame of mind.

His partially shifted hand buries into the fur and flesh. I notice blood seeping out when I advance in their direction, and before I can get there, Ben rips the wolf's esophagus from the wolf's body.

The wolf struggles before it dies, unable to take in the oxygen it needs. The sound he makes causes my stomach to roll.

Ben stands when the wolf's movements still. He turns to face me. With heavy huffs, his shoulders rise and fall. When I reach him, he takes a moment to touch the gash on my cheek, concern etching his face. His eyes travel down my body, checking for more injuries.

I grab his hand from my cheek. "I'm fine," I reassure him.

He narrows his eyes before nodding his head, satisfied with feeling my truth.

We glance around together, seeing what's left of the rogue wolves. These wolves weren't properly trained, aiming pointlessly and tiring quickly.

The Riva Pack has formidable wolves. They dispose of the bodies with swift and fluid action, raking through the scene with practiced skill. They've been trained well and I'm proud to fight by their side.

I frown while taking one more sweep of the wolves fighting before me. "Where's Flint?" I yell over the noise.

A yelp sounds beside us, and we whip our heads in that direction. Rex's red wolf rips another wolf's leg right out from under him. Blood squirts from the fresh wound. Having seen enough blood and death tonight, some at my own hands, I turn my head from the scene. I don't want to watch another death.

A spray of blood hits the tree behind me as Rex's wolf rips out his throat. The wolf goes silent.

"Flint kept going," Ben yells back.

The battle nears its end. Romaine, partially shifted, joins us, and Victoria's russet orange wolf trots beside him.

Jacob shifts back as the last wolf is dealt with. He's naked, and I avert my gaze before my jealous mate thinks my eyes are wandering. "That's the last of it."

He turns to a few of his wolves. "Do another sweep," he orders. The wolves take off, dirt mixed with blood spraying from the ground as their claws dig in for traction.

"Let's go find Flint," I say warily, unsure of what we'll find once we locate him. I don't like that my friend is out of my sight. Not when he just became himself again. I need to be there, to support him, no matter his state of mind.

Staring at all the dead bodies one last time, I turn my back to them. So much death tonight, and even though these people had created a mess . . .

Ben kisses the top of my messy blonde hair and lets me lead the way.

Flint Rockland

I breathe heavily, and wheeze on exhale. Zane's last punch had broken my ribs, and I press against them with my palms while glaring at him.

Zane and I are fairly matched. I'd be a fool to admit otherwise. I hear Jazz giggle each time Zane connects and it only fuels my rage.

Exhausted and trying desperately to preserve my energy, I decide to switch tactics and let Zane attack at his will. It hurts to move, but I grit my teeth and dance out of the way when he charges at me again. He whirls, and I shift my head to the left as he swings his fist. Again, and again he repeats the

217

same actions and tactic, and the more he misses, the sloppier he becomes.

Frustrated, he lets out a growl and tackles me. I hadn't anticipated the move and I'm too fatigued to move my entire body out of the way before his body slams into mine. The wind rushes from my lungs on impact, my ribs screaming in pain as we both hit the ground with a thud.

Breathe, breathe, breathe, I chant to myself. My wolf wants full control. I shove him down because this is my fight.

Zane growls in my face before connecting his head to my nose. The crack rings in my ears and I see stars. Pain blossoms across the bridge of my nose, my eyes water, and warm blood dribbles down my cheek from above my top lip.

His hand grips my throat. My claws dig into his arms for purchase. Blood wells from his torn skin, dripping onto my chest. I hear Irene scream in the background. I ignore it, because even though I can't breathe, even though my life is literally on the line, something nags at me – tugs at my senses.

Eyes bulging and shifting to my left, my gaze lands on . . .

There, by the tree line, is a shadowy figure.

The shadow takes shape like swirling mist on a cold spring morning. A male stands with his hands in his pockets, transparent and shimmering. The world seems to slow around me, Zane's growls becoming a distant sound. I can see the trees behind the figure, clearly making out the details in the trunks. His head of dark hair is lowered before he lifts it slightly to meet my eyes. Such sorrow in their depths, such regret. I recognize him immediately, and if I could currently breathe, my breath would have hitched in my throat.

Dyson? How is he here? Why is he transparent?

It clicks, like a lightbulb illuminating a dark closet. He's a ghost – a shade, as the witch had called them.

Breathe.

His voice echoes and bounces around in the space of my oxygen-deprived brain, as if he's actually speaking the words himself.

I love you, man.

Treat your girl right.

You're not the only one who suffers, Flint.

Time speeds back up, my confusion replaced with a renewed energy, purpose, and rage. Dyson nods his head to me once. "Live," he seems to say.

A tear rolls down my cheek, and I look back to the man choking me.

My fist connects with Zane's temple, stunning him into releasing his grip on my throat. I push him off and he falls to my side, landing on his hands and knees. I stand quickly as he shakes his head to clear his vision. By the time I'm on my feet and behind him, he lifts himself to his knees.

Did that truly happen? Did I see Dyson?

I look once more and watch his lips turn up in a smile. And then, his shade shimmers away.

I double blink before I roar. The sound rips from my chest, vibrates every bone, and tenses every muscle.

Pulling my arm back, I throw it forward with all the strength I have. My claw buries into Zane's back, slices through his skin, muscle, and bone, until it hits the thudding beat of his heart.

This heart isn't heavy and covered in thick goo. It's warm and slippery. *Beating.*

He stills his movements, crying out in pain as I wrap my fingers around the organ, but my hearing is muffled by the adrenaline thrusting through my body. My chest rises and falls with exaggeration, my eyes wide and wild.

Breathe.

Dyson's toothy grin, the extra skip in his step, and his obnoxious laugh flash before my eyes.

"Enjoy hell," I growl in Zane's ear.

In one swift motion, I yank the beating heart from his body and toss it aside. His muscles slacken and he slumps forward.

Sounds come crashing back in full force. It's like coming out of a dark tunnel and onto a busy street. Birds screech and frantically flap their wings. Fire roars and licks the tree. A soft breeze rustles the branches. The subtle noises are disorienting, almost too loud for my ears. My chest rises and falls, the pain a crippling reminder, before I turn to face Jazz.

I hear rustling in the brush behind me, and soon, Bre calls my name. I know what she wants and what she's going to say. The battle is over. And now, there's just one last, soulless life to dispose of.

I sweep my eyes over Irene. "You okay?" I ask around my canines, breathy and with much effort.

Her eyes are wide and glossy with unshed tears. She waits a moment before she nods, then blinks. A few drops of tears fall over her swollen and bruised cheek. My wolf growls, not liking that my mate is injured in any way.

Physical wounds are easier to heal than internal ones, I assure him. I know what that's like. I wouldn't wish it on anyone, especially my mate, but if the external bruises are all there is . . .

I shake my head, the pain and anger of my past and present threatening to take over.

Removing my eyes from my mate's, I stalk toward Jazz, purpose and confidence in my step. Her frightened face tells me she knows she's reached her end. I allow a small, satisfied smile.

"Nice to see you, Jazz. How was playing queen?" I ask as I cross the rest of the lawn.

She begins to back up, the heel of her shoes stumbling over the slight bumps of dirt. Grabbing a stick wrapped in flaming cloth from the ground, she waves it at me threateningly. "Stay back." The shake in her voice betrays her.

My smile grows wider. "Not a chance."

Bre appears in my peripheral vision. She quickly unties Irene from the tree. The flaming tree next to it is starting to drop its branches, threatening my mate in her captivity.

"I'm going to enjoy this. Every last fucking second of it."

Rage, love, betrayal, loss—it overwhelms me, fueling my advance, my motives. She's the reason everything happened. She's the cause of all of this.

Jazz stills her movements, fear in her eyes. She drops the torch and turns, sprinting toward the forest. In her desperate attempt for escape, she looks back at me and my grin. She pumps her arms faster, trying to get her heeled shoes to work correctly as they continue to sink in the soil with each step.

I laugh and drop the barrier I've been holding up between my wolf and me. All my feelings, all my emotions, all the events this woman has put me and my pack through, rips through me. I give it all to my wolf.

Shifting on the spot, pieces of my clothes fly into the air and scatter across the ground.

Flint Rockland's Wolf

Freedom. Rage. Revenge.

I tense my muscles, lift my head, and howl at the stars. Hearing my prey disappear into the trees, my head snaps back. My feet dig into the soil, pawing the ground. With a snarl, I push off. Dirt and chunks of grass spray behind me as I give chase. My body low to the ground, the wind tickling my fur. The scent of fear forces its way into my nose.

Closer, closer, closer.

My prey screams and I lift my lips, exposing my canines. A snarl rips from my chest, my ears flat against my head.

I leap into the air. My front paws land on my prey's back. My jaw clamps around the back of her neck, teeth sinking into the skin. Blood flows over my tongue, tasting of iron. I growl and twist my head, forcing her to the ground. We land with a thud.

Her screams force my ears to lay flat once more, the sound too loud. She wiggles, shifting my teeth. My teeth hit a vital vein. Blood sprays my face, the ground, the surrounding leaves and twigs.

She partially shifts, her wolf attempting to fight for their life. I tighten my jaw, my teeth hitting something solid. Bone.

Her claws dig into the ground, raking the dirt, gathering small piles. She moans. I growl, blinking away the sprays of blood.

One swift twist of my neck and the bone cracks between my teeth. Her noises stop.

Limp, quiet. Her heart stills, her jaw slack. The blood now just a steady flow, seeping into my mouth, onto the ground. Instinct takes over and I shake her wilted body. I snarl, blink, clench my jaw one more time.

I open my mouth and she drops to the ground. I stare at the body and bark once. The threat, gone.

My human smiles inside me, satisfied.

Freedom. We are free.

I lick my chops and feel a gentle nudge against the barrier. My human is asking to take control. I blink, unsure. He nudges again. I look once more at the corpse, shake my fur, and obey.

Bones crack. Reshape. A small whine travels through my nose. I seep, retreat back inside.

Flint Rockland

I stand upright with effort, my hand applying pressure to my broken ribs. My firm fingers try to still their movements against my harsh breaths.

The slight breeze caresses my naked body. It's calming and cool and lovely. It's over. It's truly over.

Looking down at my wolf's kill, I curl my top lip.

I choose to leave her there to rot in the forest for eternity. It's everything she deserves.

Without another look, I travel back the way my wolf came.

224

CHAPTER FIFTEEN

Evo Johnson

"It's done," I tell my mate while hanging up the phone. Ben had called. "They should be home soon." I glance back down at the bundle sleeping in my arm and press my nose to his hair, the scent comforting me in ways I never knew I needed.

So peaceful, so oblivious to the day's events. The sun peeks through the window, alerting me to a new day. But not this little one. He couldn't care less.

His tiny fists open and close, looking for something to grasp. I place my finger in it before Darla has the chance to.

Growling a soft warning at the woman who has tried everything in the book of grandparents to sneak more moments in with my son, she backs away and plops back into her chair. A heavy huff escapes her pouting lips, and she crosses her arms.

A tiny squeak comes from the bundle when my growl vibrates against him. I make a shushing sound and smile. "Coleman," I coo, calling him by his first name.

"It fits, doesn't it," Kenna says from the bed. Reese ordered her to stay off her feet, and so far, she's listened. She watches us, adoration thick in her emotions. "I figured . . . that it'd fit . . ." she trails off and a thick tear rolls down her flushed cheeks.

Coleman was Dyson's last name. I couldn't think of a better way to honor our fallen pack mate.

Cole stirs in my arms. His face scrunches and his mouth opens. A soft, velvety cry escapes and I stiffen, unsure of what to do next.

Kenna holds out her arms. "He's hungry again."

I place a kiss on his tiny, squishy forehead and breathe in his scent one more time before passing him to my mate. Her arms fold around him and I kiss away the tear from the edge of her jaw. "You're so beautiful," I tell her, because she is. In this moment, she's the most stunning woman I've ever seen.

Flint Rockland

As I hit the clearing, Irene dashes toward me. Her warm arms wrap around my bare chest and she buries her face in the crook of my neck, tears wetting the skin.

I brush her hair with my fingertips, breathe in her scent, and tilt her head back. Rubbing my fingers over her cheeks before caressing her bottom lip with my thumb, I search her wet eyes, and then bend my head to capture her mouth.

A tear escapes my own eyes. It trails down my under-eye, over my sore cheekbone, and drips from my jaw. Relief frees my emotions. She's safe. My pack is safe.

I quicken the kiss, desperate to show what I can't say, what I don't know how to say. I pour everything I'm feeling into the action and she responds the same.

Someone coughs behind Irene. I break the kiss, surveying my pack and the Riva Pack waiting there. Some have averted their gaze, some have sorrow in their eyes, and a few try out a smile.

"How many?" I ask, recognizing the grief in their eyes.

"Dead?" Ben asks. I nod. "Jessup and Evalyn are gone."

I briefly close my eyes. I didn't know them well, but they were still part of our pack.

Jacob clears his throat, his voice thick with contained emotion. "We lost two."

I breathe deep. "I'm sorry for your loss," I tell him, squeezing my arms a little tighter around my mate.

"Thank you," he replies, inclining his head.

"Who?" Irene asks Jacob, her voice muffled.

Jacob's jaw ticks. "Joseph and Chase. Cinderson is injured, but a few of ours have already taken him back to our territory. He'll be fine."

I kiss the top of Irene's head when she squeezes me a little tighter. Those were her friends who died today – people she's grown up with.

Bre turns to face the scene. "What do we do with everything?"

My eyes narrow at the shed. "Burn it."

Ben nods and begins barking orders to bring all the bodies and place them inside the shed.

"Leave Jazz where she is," I rumble. Ben glances at me, blinks in acknowledgment, and then inclines his head.

I ask Irene, "Your brother?"

A sob racks her body. "The tree."

"Shit," someone murmurs in the crowd.

"I see," I whisper to her. If I could, I'd bring Jazz back to life and kill her all over again. She hurt my mate and those she cares about.

"Are you –" I swallow. "Are you okay?" She nods against me.

A part of me is grateful Irene didn't receive the same fate. I know it's selfish to wish such a thing. We're standing near fresh corpses, for shit's sake. But in this moment, clutching my mate, I don't care. I don't care how selfish it is, because all that matters is that I don't have to bury her, too.

I glance back to the area I saw Dyson's shade, my thoughts reminding me of him and how I'll have to watch him be lowered into the ground. He didn't just save me on the Gray Pack territory. He saved me tonight, too. He reminded me to live – to move on. To pull myself together and keep fighting.

I search the area, but he's gone. *Gone.*

Maybe he was never there. It seemed so real . . . Was it a moment of weakness? A hallucination from an oxygen-deprived brain? Or was it actually real?

I don't know the answers to my questions, but I make a mental note to discuss it with Katriane. I need answers and I know she has them. She's made a believer out of me.

A half hour later, Irene cries in my chest while the pack places the bodies into the shed. When they're done, her sobs diminish to quiet hiccups.

Ben waves us over. I take Irene's hand in mine and we walk the short distance. She pauses, glancing at the charred trunk while I pick up the torch still on the ground. Rex lights it again with a lighter from his pocket.

Remaining silent, I stand with her while carefully watching her expression. Several seconds ticking by as her mind wanders. I know that feeling all too well—the shock. The devastation. A tired and distraught mind has a hard time keeping up with reality.

I give her the chance she deserves to silently say goodbye to her brother, and then, as if deciding that she needs to move on, she snaps from her trance.

Irene grabs the gas can and we continue our walk. Once reaching the entrance of the shed, we survey the bodies piled high in the makeshift living room. Irene pours the gasoline over the bodies and steps back out of the shed. I throw the torch from where I'm at and together, watch the flames engulf the pile. I turn my back from the rogues, take my mate's hand, and exit the shed.

Closing this chapter of our lives, Ben shuts the shed door behind me, metal clinking against metal. The smoke puffs out of the cracks in windows and doors and rises to the brightening sky.

CHAPTER SIXTEEN

Irene Scott

I lean against the wall, watching as Flint coos to the little baby in his arms. Cole's eyes are open, and he soaks in everything Flint whispers to him. His tiny blue eyes hang on every word, every murmur.

My heart melts, my love blossoms, and I realize that I could have missed this. I was close to missing this. My mate, our possible children, my future . . . with him.

My brother is gone, Flint's best friend is gone. Several pack mates are dead, and yet, we still stand strong. Our lives keep on moving while theirs no longer exists, sacrificed so that we may see another day. I will honor their death until my last gasping breath, but I refuse to let it stop me from living my life. I won't let that sacrifice be wasted. And with that, I let my love for this man consume me and take my breath away.

His eyes lift to mine when he feels me staring at him. I cross my arms as he holds my gaze and wonder what he's thinking.

His lips twitch into a smile. He glances at the baby and then back to me. Is he thinking about the future, too?

Flint stands from his chair next to Kenna's bed and carefully hands the baby back to Kenna. Tucking in the blanket Cole is swaddled in, he turns to me and subtly nods his head toward the door.

He leaves first, and just as I'm about to follow, Evo places his hands on my shoulder. I glance up at him and we stare at each other while he reads my emotions. I don't know what he finds there, but eventually, he smiles and squeezes my shoulder in affection. Then, he releases me.

I incline my head, thanking him because I know what this means. He's forgiven me. He's accepted me. He knows that I have nothing left to hide.

A lump forms in my throat and relief floods my system. Although I lost people, all wasn't for nothing. I get to live. I get to be free and grow old next to my mate. I get to join a pack that I've longed to be part of. Maybe it makes me selfish. Maybe it makes me a disgusting person for being grateful during such circumstances, but dwelling on it . . .

I take a deep breath, swallow the lump in my throat, and follow Flint. We descend the stairs together, and once we reach the landing, Flint grabs my hand. His palm is warm, and his touch sends tingles up my arm. He leads me to the sliding glass door. The door is new and so clear, it almost doesn't look like there's anything there.

Without a word, he opens it, and slides it shut behind me.

The outdoor air curls around my exposed arms. "Where are we going?" I ask.

He stays silent, continuing to tug me to his destination. We arrive at his quarters, and as we step inside, he grins. It's a small little grin, one that makes my toes curl with anticipation.

Latching the door quietly, he turns to me and backs me to a wall. Our breath mingles in the space between us. He lifts his hand and trails warm fingers down my cheek while his eyes memorize every detail of my face.

"If you ever do that again—if you ever try to sacrifice yourself, I – I . . ." his voice trails off, words failing him.

I place my arms around his waist and rest my head against his chest. "I won't," I whisper.

This is my mate, the one destined for me. My strength, my weakness, my entire future. I'll never break his heart by trying to leave this world on purpose. Never again.

"Good," he grunts, and in the next moment, he's picking me up.

Placing my arms around his neck, my legs hugging his torso, he carries us through his small living room and into his bedroom. I kiss him, placing all my feelings into it, and he returns with the same.

He lays me gently on the bed, his body towering over me as he breaks the kiss. His gaze searches mine and he whispers, "I love you."

Those three words could have stopped my heart. "I love you, too," I say, my voice thick with emotion.

He groans and captures my mouth again. Out of desperation, he fumbles with the bottom of my jeans before sliding them off my legs. Next, he discards his own and throws them across the room.

With one goal in mind, he skips all the foreplay, parts my folds, and slides his dick in with one, swift motion.

A gasp from the immediate intrusion hisses between my teeth, my eyelids fluttering with the sensation. We groan together before he pumps his hips. The *slap, slap, slap of skin*, the immediate pressure, the sounds of our pleasure, all encourages my excitement.

My head falls back against the mattress and I moan. My walls clamp around him, sucking him in deeper and deeper until I'm fully claimed. He shifts a bit, lifting my hips a little higher and rubbing just the right spot. I suck in a breath, the contact almost too much.

His pace quickens, and then heat builds in my lower belly with such a force that my breaths, my skin, and my muscles quiver in anticipation. He pumps faster, harder, unable to control himself. Our shared loved has turned into a desperate need – a need to be closer than we've ever been.

"Flint," his name whispers from my lips.

My breasts bounce, my nipples tight buds.

He groans again. I glance at him with hooded eyes, my body rocking underneath him to the same rhythm. His eyes glow wolf, and it encourages my own wolf to reach toward the surface. His canines elongate at the same time mine do.

"You're not going anywhere, Ira," Flint says around his teeth. "You're mine."

The admission causes the heat in my belly to explode and my orgasm hits with full force. I know that everything that follows is going to be pure instinct, and instead of shying away from it, I embrace it.

I arch my body toward Flint and sink my teeth into his neck. He groans, the sound vibrating his neck and my lips, as he reaches his climax.

He continues pumping, but he bends his head. His teeth sink into the soft flesh of my neck, and I pull my teeth from his skin, moaning as my pleasure intensifies from his bite. It builds and builds until I can no longer think straight and no longer cope.

Blackness descends.

Flint Rockland

I stand at the grave of my freshly buried pack mates. Jessup and Evalyn are next to the one I stand before. Carved across a headstone is Dyson Coleman. A picture of his face is etched into the rock, his cheerful smile a painful reminder of his jolly laugh I remember so well. Sometimes, when the wind blows just right, I swear I can hear that laughter.

He's buried, six feet under my feet, and I can't help but feel that it's my fault. I disappeared from his life. If I hadn't done that, if I would have remained a loyal friend, perhaps Dyson would still be alive and I could hear his voice once more.

Irene steps up beside me, her black dress blowing in the breeze, and takes my hand in hers. "It's not your fault," she says.

I glance at her, the fresh claiming mark evidence of our union. She feels my feelings through our mating bond and has come to comfort her grieving mate.

"How is it not?" I ask around the lump in my throat.

"Dyson made a choice. You didn't make that choice for him. He wanted to save you the only way he knew how. He loved his friend." She glances back at the grave. "His plan didn't go the way he wanted, and he did the only thing left he knew to do. Dyson will be honored, he will be remembered, and he will always be loved." She glances back at me, waiting a moment before she continues, "Recognize the things you can change, Flint, and don't hold on to the things you can't."

A part of me believes her, but another part of me will always grieve him – will always blame myself.

On my other side, Evo's shadow stretches as he steps closer. He's been silent until now, as speechless as me. Does he blame himself, too? Does he think there's things he could have done differently?

He grips my shoulder. "C'mon," he says.

We're having a pack run to honor our fallen pack mates, a tradition carried down through history. Irene has agreed to join the pack and has already made the arrangements with Jacob for a smooth transition. Jacob was mad at her for a while, especially since she didn't go to him when she found herself in trouble, but ultimately, he forgave her. Kenna and Evo hold no blame to her, either. They adore her and respect her sacrifice to save their child and pack, even if that wasn't her original plan.

Kelsey and Jeremy have returned. At first, Kelsey was ripe with anger, and then her anger turned to anguish. They stuck to the inside of their quarters for a few days, grieving together and accepting what has happened in their absence. I suppose we all feel a little blame. And maybe Irene is right. Maybe it's normal to feel this way. Maybe we're not supposed to feel anything but great sorrow and deep regrets.

A howl sounds in the distance and Irene squeezes my hand. She takes off her dress and begins to shift. The most stunning brown fur sprouts from her skin before a wolf stands where she once did. Her wolf rubs against my leg, a gesture of comfort, and then she takes off after our pack.

I look back at Dyson's etched face one last time, bend down, and run my fingers over it. "I love you," I whisper to him.

Wherever he is, if he's even listening anymore, I hope to see him again someday.

EPILOGUE

Kelsey Rylend

Jeremy glances at the stick, trying to decipher the lines and what they mean.

I curse, impatient with his idiocy. "I'm pregnant," I blurt before he can discover for himself.

He grins at me, a brilliant and rare smile that lifts his rosy cheeks. The air is nearly knocked from my lungs when he abruptly lifts me into the air. We've wanted to grow a family for years and the day has finally come. It feels so surreal. I don't know if I should cry or celebrate . . . or both.

He twirls me once, my long red hair covering our faces, and I let out a squeal of excitement.

"We're going to be parents," he says, holding me close in his arms.

He sets me on my feet and drops to his knees. His cheek rests against my stomach. "Hi, baby," he coos, and my heart swells.

Being around Cole has made him soft, but this rare show of complete raw adoration . . . well, it makes me fall for him all over again.

I place my hands on my hips, fully aware I'm ruining the moment. "You know he . . . she . . .," I pause, frowning, "it can't hear you yet, right?"

He lifts his head and smiles wickedly at me. I grin back and push my hand through his hair. This man was made for me.

"I'm going to be a father," he whispers.

Flint Rockland

It's midsummer, a few months after the passing of my friend. My mate is running her errands—she went to visit Kat at her shop, picking up remedies to help Cole sleep at night. She's fitting in nicely with the pack—a great addition that makes me so proud. It's almost like she's always been here.

I sit by the water with Kenna and Bre. Evo, Ben, Jeremy, and Cole are in the backyard. They're doing everything they can to wear Cole out in hopes he'll take a little nap this afternoon.

Romaine had asked Irene if he could tag along to the shop. Irene had refused, for which I'm grateful. An unmated male around my female isn't something I was ready to deal with yet. So instead, he had planted himself on a chair on the back porch, and now, I can hear him laugh at the men trying to overpower a baby.

Truly, I don't blame them for their efforts. The kid is adorable, but his cries in the middle of the night can be heard in mine and Irene's quarters. I hold great sympathy for his tired parents.

Victoria is running patrol, while Kelsey and Darla mess around in the kitchen concocting who knows what. Food experiments have been their hobby lately, with the pack being the guinea pigs and unwilling taste-testers to whatever they concoct.

Life has seemingly returned to normal, but there's still that one piece missing from all our lives, a gaping hole in the pack link that Dyson once filled.

Bre leans against one of my shoulders while Kenna leans against the other. We sit quietly, content with the peace that nature has to offer. The day is hot, and the bugs are bothersome. We swat at them every now and again, hoping to stave them off, but they're persistent.

The silence stretches until I feel a wetness dripping down my arm. I glance down at Kenna and grimace as her drool slips past her open mouth. *She's asleep!*

I squirm, trying to get Kenna off. She and Bre both startle to my movements and wildly look around.

"What?" Kenna asks, eyes wide in panic. "Is the baby okay?"

"You were drooling down my arm," I grumble, trying to wipe it off on my shorts.

Bre sighs next to me and turns back to the water.

"Shit," Kenna says, wiping the side of her mouth with the back of her hand. "I didn't mean to fall asleep."

I eye her out of the corner of my eye, pretending offense. She shoves my shoulder mockingly, but there's a smile spreading over her tired face.

"So, what now?" Bre asks in a quiet voice.

I frown. "What do you mean?"

"You gonna have kids someday?"

My shoulders rise and fall. "Maybe. We haven't really talked about it."

She nods solemnly.

Kenna leans forward and looks at Bre. "What about you and Ben?"

She mimics my shrug, but eventually smiles at the thought. "I wouldn't mind seeing a few miniature Bens running around."

I scoff. "That's exactly what we need. Several mini-Bens and Bres barking orders."

Kenna giggles while trailing a finger over a small rock. "Can you imagine what they'll be like once they talk? All the demands a little person could ask for. It'll be funny as hell, watching Ben trying to gather his pups and make them listen."

Bre joins her giggles. "Yeah, it would."

The girls sigh dreamily while I fantasize about what it'd be like to hold my child for the first time. To be a part of growing a tiny baby, smelling the top of its head, hearing him or her call me daddy.

A smile spreads across my face, too. I didn't think I'd ever get this, let alone want it. But now that I have the opportunity, new possibilities are making me see the light. I want more. I want a family. And with Irene, I can have it all.

Irene Scott

I drum my fingers on the counter of Lunaire, waiting for Kat to come back in from taking out the shop's trash.

Right when I came through the front door, she asked me to man the counter while she completed some tasks. I agreed, but I knew she was using this time to avoid me. She has to know why I came here.

She enters the store through the back door and walks behind the counter. No customers are in, which is normal for this hour of the day.

Giving me a perky smile, she asks, "What's up?"

I raise an eyebrow and fully stand up, my drumming fingers dropping to my side. "I need a few herbs for Cole. He isn't sleeping. Do you have anything for that?"

She continues her smile while holding up a finger. "I have just the thing."

Walking around the counter, she heads to the herbal shelf. Knowing exactly what she's going for, she carefully picks up the tiny glass bottle and it clinks against its contained neighboring herbs. She turns and places it in my hand. The label is in French, a language I don't understand.

"This will do the trick?" I ask, turning the small bottle over and examining its purple contents.

"Yep," she says while heading to the register.

I give her the bottle and she rings it up. She tells me the total and I grab the wad of cash from my pocket and hand it over.

"What are you?" I ask bluntly.

She cringes. Shutting the drawer with a sigh, she turns to face me. "I knew that question was coming," she mumbles.

I take the small bag she had placed the purple herbs in. "Is it why the coven disowned you?"

"Yes," she says softly. "Sort of. Not really. Actually—" She scratches her neck. "I really shouldn't discuss it." Her hands move to the hem of her black shirt, fumbling with the end.

I feel like she's a broken record, repeating the same answers she did that night a few months ago. I thought the space would have helped her feel more inclined to tell me, but it would seem I'm wrong in my assessment. Maybe we aren't as close as I thought we were.

My jaw ticks as my patience wears thin. I stand in silence for a few moments before lowering my voice. "What are you, Kat? What happened?"

"I can't tell you."

I tilt my head back, stare at the ceiling, and rub my neck with my free hand. "All right," I say, resigning to the fact that maybe there's a reason. Everyone has secrets. Maybe hers scares her into silence. I glance back at her. "Can I ask one more question?"

Her eyes narrow. "I can't promise an answer."

"Are you more than a witch?"

Her body remains still as she weighs her options of trusting me or sending me on my way. Finally, she answers, "Yes."

I nod, satisfied to have some kind of answer.

"Someday—" I begin.

"Someday, I'll tell you." Her tongue darts out to lick the corner of her lips. "When it's safe."

I eye her suspiciously, now suddenly worried for my friend's safety. So, it is fear that makes her bite her tongue. Whatever secret she's keeping, it terrifies her.

"That'll have to do for now," I mumble. I turn to leave, and when I'm a few feet away from the counter, I stop in my tracks.

"Ira?" Kat calls. "What is it?"

I turn toward hers but keep my eyes lowered to the ground. "Flint told me something a few weeks ago," I begin.

"Okay . . ." Kat says, confusion dipping her tone.

"He said," I pause. "He said he saw Dyson after he was dead."

Kat remains silent and I glance back at her. Her eyes hold so much fright.

"What do you mean?"

"During the battle . . . there was a moment where he was losing his fight. He said Dyson came but he wasn't whole. What was the word he used?" I ponder aloud while scanning the shelves.

My eyes flicker back to Kat and I see her gulp. "A shade?" she asks softly.

The lightbulb goes off and my eyebrows flicker up for a split second. "That's the one. Do you know anything about that?"

She hesitates, until finally, she says, "Do you remember the story around the bonfire?" I nod. "Shades don't live in this realm. They shouldn't be able to cross over . . . not anymore." Her eyes flicker back and forth across the glass counter, seeing nothing as she frantically works through her mind.

"Kat?" I whisper. Goosebumps rise over my skin. "You okay?"

She chews the inside of her lip before forcing a nod. "I'll look into it," she says.

Satisfied, I nod. Waving goodbye to her, I leave the store, hoping my friend isn't into something deep. I know witches can have an evil side, using dark and forbidden magic. God, if she's messing with that . . .

The door chimes as Irene walks out. I stare at her back, my mind working frantically to what she's told me. Shades don't belong here. They haven't been able to cross realms since Myla, the first born witch, died a few hundred years ago. The few that are here—the photographed ones—are stuck. There's a reason why they're all dressed from that era. But new ones? Ones that are freshly dead?

Something's wrong. This shouldn't be happening. They shouldn't be able to leave the Death Realm. Something's shifted, gone wrong, wavering the boundaries that are set to keep the two realms a part, and with good reason.

I finally blink when Irene enters her car, a distracted look on her face as she drives out of my small parking lot. Their pack is still healing, that much is clear. Such a death toll can do that to anyone, and from what I hear, they didn't exactly have it easy before the Rogue Battle.

That's what the supernatural world is calling it: The Rogue Battle. It'll go down in our histories as a legend.

A Rogue Pack has never existed before. They're usually feared individually, and together, they should be a nightmare. For two packs to join together and kill the miscreants . . . that's unheard of. Things are changing – so many things. I'm just glad Irene came out of it alive.

I had an internal war with myself about trusting Irene with my secret. She would keep it. I know she would. But the more who know . . .

The only people who know about it are those of my coven. My ex-coven, I guess. It's what happens when you dabble with the wrong person. It's what happens when anyone bargains with the Fee.

I should have known that begging the Fee to save my coven would come at a price. A steep price. One with dark magic I can't control and can't ignore. And I was an idiot for making that bargain – was an idiot for thinking the price of it wouldn't be so steep.

Now, my coven wants nothing to do with me. I broke their laws to save their lives, and they cast me out.

Sighing, submitting myself to my fate of a coven-less life, I grab a rag and clean the fingerprint smudges from the counter Irene left behind.

Something is coming. I can sense the shift across the realms – feel it ripple right into this shop. It makes my bones itch.

I glance outside once more and watch a car pass by. I'd love to know what my role in it all is, because the Fee don't grant their powerful magic to just anyone. There's a reason they said yes to me – a reason they gave me a cure for my coven's illness. I just know it.

Time will tell. It always does. And that scares the shit out of me.

ABOUT THE AUTHOR

D. Fischer is a mother of two busy boys, a wife to a wonderful and supportive husband, and an owner of two hyper, sock-loving dogs and an attention-seeking fat cat named Geralt. Together, they live in Orange City, Iowa.

Follow D. Fischer on Instagram, Facebook, Amazon, Bookbub, and Email.

www.dfischerauthor.com

ALSO BY D. FISCHER

| THE CLOVEN PACK SERIES |

| RISE OF THE REALMS SERIES |

| HOWL FOR THE DAMNED SERIES |

|HEAVY LIES THE CROWN SERIES

| NIGHT OF TERROR SERIES |

| GRIM FAIRYTALE COLLECTION |

Made in the USA
Las Vegas, NV
29 November 2020